A
STATUES

Anne Stevenson

A FAWCETT CREST BOOK

Fawcett Publications, Inc., Greenwich, Connecticut

A GAME OF STATUES

THIS BOOK CONTAINS THE COMPLETE TEXT OF THE
ORIGINAL HARDCOVER EDITION.

A Fawcett Crest Book reprinted by arrangement with
G. P. Putnam's Sons.

Library of Congress Catalog Card Number: 71-175255

Printed in the United States of America
August 1974

To Camilla Shaw

A GAME
OF
STATUES

❧ 1 ❧

BEFORE LONG it would be dawn, and then she could sleep. She had done very well yesterday: nearly three hours, from four to seven. She might be as lucky as that again today. And then next week it would begin to get better. She was sure of that; she was counting on it. It had been the same on the first anniversary, and then it had got better. When they moved here, she had given up the sleeping pills and she wasn't going back to them. She didn't mind being awake here. It was a peaceful house. And it was amazing how little sleep you needed to keep going.

She turned in the wide double bed, the bed Mrs. Sendall had bestowed on her with that odd mixture of apology and comradeship. Widows both, she had appeared to be saying, we are entitled to our lonely symbols of our former state, and besides, we are used to them. It takes practice to be comfortable in a single bed after years of stretching and rolling in all that familiar space.

"I haven't a single bed in the house," she had announced. "Except in the attic. The maids, poor little things, had very narrow iron things. I expect they're still

9

stacked up there somewhere. When this house was furnished in my grandfather's day, it was nothing but big beds. Of course, as I said, if you wanted to bring your own furniture, my dear. . . ."

Ginny had reassured her. She had sold it all, not in that first instinctive overwhelming impulse to be rid of such frequent sources of pain that had led to the packaging up of all of her husband's clothes and personal belongings, down to his cuff links and lighter, and their dispatch to the Salvation Army, but in the cooler, more calculated attitude of a two-year-old grief. It had been simply that if she stayed in that house with their furniture in their rooms, looking out at that patch of garden and the garage where the car had been kept, then she would go mad. She could feel herself going mad, a strange, subtle process, a forced calm above an inner hysteria. So she had accepted Mrs. Sendall's offer and moved in, bringing nothing but a trunkful of belongings and her small son.

Even Ben had his own double bed. They had put a bolster down it the first night to make it smaller for him, but by the second night he had thrown it out. Like his father, he liked a lot of room.

Outside, the birds had begun their dawn chorus. Ginny put on her dressing gown and went along the corridor to her son's room. He lay, sunk heavily in slumber, looking as if he had been struck asleep in the middle of a fight, bedclothes thrown back, one arm flung wide, the small hand barely relaxed from a clenched fist. His face bore the complete and irresistible innocence of all sleeping children. His mouth was slightly open, and there was a faint frown on his forehead. As Ginny watched him, he trembled like a dog dreaming on the hearthrug before a fire. She wondered what dreams were troubling him. She bent forward and drew the bedclothes over him, curving his arms back into the warm nest of the bed. Moving here had been good for him, she was sure. He was no longer white. There was a soft color in his cheeks. This wonder-

ful, extraordinary summer was already beginning to tan
him. This was the first week of his holiday. By the end of
six weeks he would be as healthy as any. No pneumonia
this winter, no nights sitting by his bedside, terrified of
his breathing.

On the bedside table was the book Mrs. Sendall had
given him for his birthday. Ginny picked it up. On the
flyleaf he had written: "This book belongs to John Benson, eight years old." There followed their address, the
town, the county, "England, Europe, The World, The
Universe, Space." Space had been written in block capi-
tals and underlined in red. Next to the book lay a small
collection of his treasures, the things he had happened to
have in his pockets that day. There was a matchbox containing the brown chrysalis of some unidentified insect
that he had been patiently waiting to turn into a butterfly
for more than a week now. There was a black pebble, a
piece of thick green bottle glass, a fragment of blue and
white crockery, a dead spider, two rubber bands, a piece
of twig of unknown but manifest significance, a stub of
pencil, and the present pride of his life, the big double-
bladed safety penknife his grandfather had sent him,
which contained all the appropriate attachments for
opening bottles and removing stones from horses' hooves.

Ginny smiled. She wanted to kiss him but was afraid
she might wake him. She never made use of him for comfort when he was awake. But when he was asleep, that,
she thought, was forgivable. She drew the small wooden
chair close to the bed and sat down beside him, enclosing
herself for a while in a circle of warmth and tenderness
and love.

It was going to be another beautiful day. Mrs. Sendall,
dressed in a short checked gingham dressing gown, nicely
crisp and starched, opened her bedroom window and
gazed out over the garden. It stretched as far as, with her
short sight, she could see, and then beyond it were the al-

lotments that no one bothered to use anymore and the
abandoned church and finally the tidal creek that wound
its narrow way into the river and the sea. No wonder they
all said this part of the town was like being in the heart of
the country. It had been the country when she was young,
and still, in the summer months, the house took on the air
of its old days. Trees dense with leaf fanning out in exu-
berant bursts of green framed its views and shaded its
walks, forming a barrier against reality in much the same
way as the distance between the windows of Mrs. Sendall's room and the gardens it overlooked sustained the
illusion of ordered substance. But in fact the lushness was
that of desolation. The hedges in the rose garden were
misshapen with untrimmed growth. The grass grew wild,
except for the small patch she and Ginny had cut themselves, pushing and shoving the ancient lawn mower
through a seemingly endless meadow, with many heaves
and sighs and stops to clear the blades of slaughtered
dandelions. The white convolvulus greedily entwined its
clinging fingers around bushes, flowers, and walls alike,
and ants built tall palaces in the neglected tennis courts.
The roses looked beautiful, and their scent filled the evening; but they were spreading like plump women past
their prime, full-blown, too heavy, bending to the ground
on weak and thorny stalks, their soft hearts swarming
with insects.

It should have been a sad garden, symbolic of decay
and a life near its close, but to Mrs. Sendall it was not
sad. It was friendly and full of character and springing
with life under the unexpected sun. The pigeons cooed in
the tall trees, and the small birds chattered and sang and
cried warnings when Alice the cat appeared, to stalk lazily along the mellowed brick walls, stretching her paws out
and moving her tail languidly.

She was there now, a blurred figure on the end wall,
coming sedately home from whatever orgiastic delights

the night had encompassed. Following her unvarying custom, she would now curl up under the peach tree and sleep soundly, until seven o'clock and the sound of the kettle being filled for breakfast brought her in.

Mrs. Sendall picked up the binoculars to take a closer look at her. Taking a closer look at things was one of the habits of solitude Mrs. Sendall had developed, first begun when she had come across her husband's racing glasses at the bottom of a tin trunk and, peering out of the window through them with mild curiosity before putting them away again, found all the most elusive and interesting bits of the landscape come leaping into her sight. After that, she spent many hours gazing with quiet enjoyment at the involved and intricate life of the garden.

Anyone seeing her, she reflected, would no doubt think her a nosy old woman; a dotty one, too, she wouldn't be surprised. She would, if she saw anyone training binoculars on her. Perhaps she ought to stop now that Ginny and Ben were here. Imagine anyone saying to Ben, "You live in that house where that mad old woman lives. I've seen her, staring out of her window for hours on end. . . ." Only, of course, the nice thing was there was no one to see her. No houses, not even the ugly little blocks of flats Mr. Morgan had built all over poor Enid Watson's garden the moment he had got her out and pulled her house down, overlooked Mrs. Sendall's garden. You could only really see anything of the house from the allotments, and not many people worked those anymore. They either had their own gardens to grow vegetables in or preferred to buy them from the shops. At one time, these small oblong pieces of land each divided from its neighbor by either narrow paths or more simply a stick or stone to mark the boundary, had been in great demand. The town council owned the land and let out the patches to local tenants to grow vegetables or flowers on. During the war Mrs. Sendall remembered it had been a hive of industry, a flourishing market garden full of toiling figures every summer evening. Growing food hadn't been a pastime then; it had been a necessity.

She raised the glasses and focused on Alice, noting behind the cat and blending very nicely with her tortoiseshell coat an unusual purple flower that seemed to be spreading over the wall from the other side. She had better go down and identify it later. It might turn out to be poisonous, and then she would have to warn Ben about it. Of course, it might not be a weed. It might be something more interesting like runner beans running wild or cabbages mutating; only their flowers were the wrong color. More likely something like kale. Had anyone been growing kale? She moved the glasses to take in the allotments and was sweeping slowly across them with quite an accomplished smoothness of movement when something bright flashed a painful reflection across her eyes. She jerked the glasses down and rubbed her eyes. Then she focused the binoculars back on the same place.

She had missed him the first time, but there he was. The same man as yesterday. Just standing there. He must have seen her looking at him yesterday because he had come nearer, nearer the shelter of the wall that divided the garden from the allotments. He might think he was out of sight, but from this height she could see him perfectly well. He was lighting a cigarette. The flash had been the sun catching the lighter as he took it out of his pocket. He had his hands cupped around the cigarette, hiding his face. Now he was turning away. How irritating! Yesterday he had been too far away to see his face clearly, and now he wouldn't stand still long enough to have a good look. She didn't need a look to know who it was, though. It was really too bad. It was an intrusion of privacy, and she would say so loud and clear. Yes, it was too bad. It was enough to spoil the morning for her.

She put away the binoculars and, going to the dressing table, began to take out her curlers. "Cissie, my girl," she told her reflection. "You've got to face the fact that there's another siege coming.

"Wretched people," she said, brushing her hair vigorously. "Why can't they leave the poor old place alone?"

Every school holiday before this, Ginny had given up whatever temporary job she had taken in order to be with Ben. This was the first time she had risked working through the holiday. It was Mrs. Sendall who had finally persuaded her.

"I'm here all the time," she said. "I can keep an eye on him. I've looked after small boys before. It's worth trying, isn't it? If you get worried or Ben starts fretting, you can give in your notice and come back. But I think it's a pity to give up a job you like."

Ben hadn't said anything. It was all strange to him: the new house, the new surroundings, the fact that they had moved away from his friends and his school and that he would be going to a new school in September. Ginny didn't know if she was doing the best or the worst thing for him, whether a time of change was the right time to introduce a new factor into their lives, or if she should remain close to him. Anyway, she was risking it, and so far it seemed to be working. They were giving her a week's holiday at the shop even though she had been with them such a short time, and that was going to help. She was going to take it right at the end of Ben's holiday so she would have those days with him before he had to plunge into the adventure of the new school.

When she came down to the kitchen after her breakfast, all ready to leave, Ben was tucking into his cornflakes, his weekly comic propped up against the milk jug. The cat was crouched by her plate, head on one side, chewing with absorbed concentration, and Mrs. Sendall, her small feet in their neat pink slippers resting on the rungs of Ben's chair, was drinking her fourth cup of tea and reading the strip cartoons in the morning paper. The kitchen window was open to the garden. It was already very hot.

"Time for another cup?" Mrs. Sendall asked. She folded her newspaper and tapped Ben on the shoulder with it. "Pass the milk jug, Ben." He passed the jug across to her obediently, and she poured Ginny a cup of tea.

"I've found the answer to the problem," she said. "Look." It was a whistle. "I knew there was one somewhere. From the time when my husband used to referee matches. We've worked out signals, haven't we, Ben?"

Ben nodded. He was very impressed by Mrs. Sendall. He had never met anyone like her before. She treated him as if he were only a year or so younger than herself.

"It was no use me yelling myself hoarse," Mrs. Sendall went on. "He never heard me, but he'll hear this. We've been practicing. Listen." She blew a short sharp blast on the whistle. The cat leaped away from its plate, fur on end, and Ben collapsed in giggles. He jumped off his chair and chased Alice around the kitchen. He got his hands on her, but she slithered desperately out of his grasp and shot through the cat door so fast she left a scattering of hairs behind her.

"You should leave that poor animal alone," Ginny said. "You'll frighten her to death. But I think the whistle is a marvelous idea."

Mrs. Sendall winked at her. Then she stood up and, coming over to Ginny, took her hands in hers and gave her a little kiss on the cheek. Her skin was very soft, and she smelled delightful. "Don't worry, dear," she said. "Have a good day." Her sleepless nights, Ginny realized, must be showing in her face.

"Thank you," she said. "Ben, are you coming to the gate with me?"

He ran ahead of her down the curved drive to the front gate. He was a nice-looking little boy, she thought. He wasn't a baby any longer. The softness of the six- and seven-year-old was gone. You could already see what he would be like as a man. Not exactly like the father from whom he had taken his nickname, but of the same general type: fairly tall with dark brown hair and a good straight nose and eyes that sometimes looked blue and sometimes gray. She had put clean jeans and T-shirt out for him this morning, and although he had put them on, which was a minor triumph in itself, they already looked as if he'd been wearing them for a week. He ran from side to side in a zigzag out of sheer enjoyment of the morning, emitting almost incidentally an earsplitting zooming noise indicating his make of engine. At the gate they met the postman.

"You can save me a journey," he said, and gave a letter to Ben. From the direction of the house came the faint blast of a whistle.

"Is that Mrs. Sendall signaling you?" Ginny asked.

He nodded.

"What are you supposed to do?"

He counted solemnly on his fingers. "One whistle, don't go too far away. Two whistles, she wants to tell me something. Three whistles, food's ready."

"Well, that seems quite clear," Ginny said. "You'd better go and give her her letter. See you this evening." He nodded and went rushing off back down the drive.

She walked along the lane toward the main road, where she was to catch her bus. The postman walked with her as far as the next house, wheeling his bicycle.

"You're miles from nowhere here," he said chattily. "You ought to get a car."

"A bicycle would be more my line," Ginny said. "I'll have to get you to give me a lift on yours."

"I'll get a new saddle put on specially," he said. He was a middle-aged man with glasses. A family man. She liked all the people she had met here. They were all very friendly. There was really nothing to worry about.

Mrs. Sendall was doing out the bedrooms. She had her

routine, and she took pleasure in sticking to it. She enjoyed having someone to clear up after again, after twelve months of being on her own. It was very tedious keeping a house tidy for no one but yourself and the mice. After her husband died, she had tried taking in lodgers, but they turned out to be such an odd lot it had put her off. She seemed to get a succession of spinsterly bachelors and decaying aunts. The women were all struggling to survive on inadequate pensions, and the men wore thick woolen socks and thought a good deal about catching cold.

It was inevitable, she realized after a while. In a town such as this, with no university or big industrial complex to bring in the young and unattached in search of digs, where the young people either left for London and pastures new or lived with their parents until they married, who else would be wanting furnished rooms and meals but the failures and the dispossessed? It made her very depressed. Most of them were a good deal younger than she was but had about as much life left in them as a set of Egyptian mummies. They were all a lot too sorry for themselves. Mrs. Sendall couldn't stand people who didn't fight back. If they had tried taking each other to bed, she would have thought more of them, but they were too self-absorbed to have any such outward emotions as compassion or desire. She was very glad to see the back of them.

Then, after a few months of blissful peace and quiet, the house began to worry her. Not because she was lonely in it, but because empty rooms seemed such a waste. It was then she had the bright idea of approaching Virginia Benson.

She had noticed Ginny as soon as the girl started working in the shop. It was the best dress shop in the neighborhood, and Mrs. Sendall thought Virginia the most sympathetic person they had ever had working there. She looked very pale and fragile and at times almost overwhelmingly tired, but she was always cheerful.

There was an "air" about her, resulting from the combination of that pale hair and those delicate features with what Mrs. Sendall suspected was a rare indomitability of spirit. Mrs. Sendall felt instinctively that she was one of the tough ones, the ones who didn't say much or even do very much but who against all odds and against all misfortune stubbornly survived.

It was the owner of the shop who told her what she knew of Ginny's history. Mrs. Sendall knew the owner from her days as chairwoman of the local women's society. It was one of the reasons she first started visiting the shop; it was one of the reasons she and her friends had such license there. Mrs. Sendall often met her girlfriends there. They made quite an afternoon of it, trooping in after a lunch at the Copper Kettle and trying things on until teatime. Mrs. Sendall often thought how they must look to the assistants: plump, aging ladies, all of them nearer seventy than sixty, with too much time on their hands and a tendency to giggle like oversize schoolgirls. She liked Ginny's kindness to them. They were all pretty ridiculous old things, but Ginny never made fun of them, not even by so much as a glance or a raised shoulder. It took kindness to avoid so easy a target.

"I hear you have a long journey to get here every day," she remarked to her one day.

"It's not too bad," Ginny said. "It's only worrying if I miss the bus back to the village. You can't expect small boys to stay put in school if you're late fetching them."

"Forgive me if I sound impertinent," Mrs. Sendall said, "but couldn't you get a job nearer home?"

"I wish I could," Ginny said. "But I'm not a very satisfactory employee. I have to put Ben first. He hasn't been very well; he's had an upsetting time." She took an imperceptible breath. "His father was killed, you see. I have to watch him rather carefully. He'll be all right," she added quickly, defensively. "He's a very normal little boy. But he likes me around."

"Of course." Mrs Sendall found herself speaking then almost without her volition; the invitation came to her lips as if it was something she had been thinking about for weeks. Perhaps she had, subconsciously. "If you ever want to make a move, do let me know. I've got an old house with plenty of room. You and your son could come as paying guests, just as long as you liked. I'm quite good as a landlady, and there's a nice jungle of a garden."

Ginny had looked at her with a faint air of surprise as if she had suddenly changed from being a flat figure in a mural to three-dimensional size. She's not really with us yet, poor girl, Mrs. Sendall thought. Dear me, she shouldn't be living on her own; now that could be dangerous.

She hadn't repeated her invitation; she had let the thought of it simmer away in Ginny's mind, and two weeks later Ginny had met her by chance in the street and with an air of almost explosive decision had asked if it was still all right for her and Ben to come.

"Of course!" Mrs Sendall felt a little as if she'd lured a couple of deer out of the forest. But once decided, Ginny didn't waste time. Her house was put in the hands of an agent, her furniture was disposed of, and she and Ben were climbing out of a taxi at Mrs. Sendall's front door before she'd hardly had time to spring-clean their rooms. She hadn't regretted that impulsive invitation one bit. It was always best to rely on instinct. Whenever she had done something according to strict logic and reason, it had always gone wrong.

She unplugged the vacuum and moved along from Ginny's room to Ben's. On the way she paused by the window in the corridor to look for him. His position in the garden was announced by Alice as clearly as if she'd been holding a signpost in her paw. She was poised on top of the wall by the tennis court, head all sharp attention, tail moving slightly, swishingly from side to side. Below her the bushes stirred, and Ben's back in his yellow

T-shirt showed fleetingly for a moment as he stalked his way on elbows and stomach toward the allotments.

His bedroom was already tidy. Ginny had almost an obsession about causing work for her landlady. Mrs. Sendall swept the long brush along the curtain rail and flicked a duster across the walls before getting down to the serious polishing of floor and furniture. It was underneath Ben's bed that she found the cigarette. She took it out of the dustpan and studied it. It was a stub about two inches long. It looked as if it had been thrown away half smoked rather than stubbed out. Serve him right, she thought. But why keep it? She answered her own question. He had probably pinched it out when it made him feel sick and stuffed it in his pocket, then when he did his nightly turning out of the treasures in his pocket, the incriminating stub had rolled under the bed and been forgotten.

She sat on the bed. Now what was she to do? Tell Ginny? Lambaste Ben with a few well-chosen words? Where on earth had he got it? It was an expensive make with a fancy filter and a thin gold band around the paper about an inch down. She'd like to get her hands on whoever went about handing cigarettes to eight-year-old boys. He wouldn't have bought it, surely? Well, of course, he might. He could have got it out of a slot machine. In which case there would be a packet of them about, and was she going to go against her deepest principles and start looking through somebody else's private belongings? No, she wasn't. Not yet. It wasn't as if it were marijuana. All small boys smoked cigarettes at some time or other. She'd keep her eyes open for further signs of debauchery. She dropped the stub back in the dustpan and got on with her work.

At eleven she went downstairs and made a cup of coffee. She poured lemon squash out for Ben and opened the cake tin. She blew the whistle three times and waited to see what would happen. He came running in as pleased as Punch. She had forgotten boys of eight enjoyed codes and signals and anything that smelled of secret societies.

"Have you found any more anthills?" she asked.

He shook his head.

"When my husband was alive, that tennis court was the pride of his life. If there was so much as a fallen leaf on it, he'd jump up and down he'd get so cross."

Ben thought of an old man with a long white beard jumping up and down. He began playing the game they'd started between them. "What did your husband do, Mrs. Sendall?"

"He was a big-game hunter," she said.

"Did he shoot lions?"

"Now and again."

"And tigers?"

"Not very often."

"He wasn't really a big-game hunter, was he?" Ben said.

"No, I can't deceive you, Ben; he was not. Not what you'd really call a professional big-game hunter."

"What did he really do then?"

"He was a deep-sea diver."

He stared at her. "I don't believe *that!*"

Her straight face cracked. He looked so indignant. She began to laugh. Then Ben caught it from her, and she had to give him more lemon squash and another piece of cake to calm him down.

Ginny had her coffee in the small room at the back of the shop that did duty as office, cloakroom, and kitchen for members of the staff. There were three members of staff besides the owner, Mrs. Levison-Wrightly. There was the solid, capable fifty-year-old Mrs. Craig, who never minded how hard she worked as long as she had time off to shop for her husband's dinner. There was Eileen, who was twenty and engaged and was planning her wedding and the furnishing of her flat with all the ruthless competence of an ambitious general, and there was Ginny, who had now been working there for more than three months, almost a record for her.

"I do believe the man's actually getting up enough nerve to come in." Eileen was peering through the open door to the main shop door. At the counter, Mrs. Craig was sorting through a new batch of scarves.

"What man?" Ginny leaned back in the stiff chair and thought about closing her eyes. Sitting down had made her suddenly feel very tired.

"That good-looking one I told you about yesterday. He looked through the windows and almost came in, then changed his mind."

Ginny smiled. "You must have frightened him off."

"Thanks very much. It wouldn't have been me. Her ladyship was on the counter all yesterday afternoon. Enough to put Sir Galahad off."

Ginny glanced idly through into the shop. "Well, Mrs. Craig's there now. She wouldn't frighten anyone."

She caught a glimpse of the man, a vague shape in the doorway. Then the need to close her eyes overcame her. Five minutes of her coffee break left. Enough time to go right off into blissful darkness.

She awoke abruptly with the feeling that she was being watched. She opened her eyes. The man who had been outside the shop was now inside. He was standing by the door of the room, looking in at her. Eileen had disappeared.

He was good-looking, as Eileen had said, in a tall, loose-jointed, particularly English way. His hair was thick and fair and a bit wild, and he looked as if he ought to be wearing tweeds in a 1930's film. He was saying apologetically, "I wonder if you could help me. . . ."

Ginny stood up, annoyed at being caught asleep. She said, "One of the others. . . ."

He interrupted. "I'm afraid they're busy. I'm so sorry. I

didn't mean to disturb you." He began backing away. There was a certain clumsy charm about the way he moved, the discomfiture of a large man trapped in a feminine ambience.

"Oh. . . ." She was unaware of the exasperated kindness of her expression as she came forward to rescue him. "Of course I'll help you if I can. What were you looking for?"

He was, it gradually became apparent, looking for a present for a niece. The age of the niece presented him with some temporary difficulty. He eventually decided on sixteen.

"They grow so," he said rather helplessly. "Don't you find that? One moment they're brought to visit you in prams, and the next thing you know they're taller than you are."

His manner was engaging.

"Is she your only niece?" she asked.

"Yes, thank God. No," he added, "I shouldn't say that. She's a very nice girl, they tell me. As long as she doesn't descend on Uncle, I'm happy to send her presents twice a year.

Ginny smiled. "Don't you like relatives descending on you?"

"I don't like anyone descending on me. Neither do you, do you?"

She was slightly taken aback by this directness. She asked more coolly what sort of present he wanted to buy.

"Heaven knows," he declared. "You choose." He caught sight of the tumbled mass of scarves Mrs. Craig had had to leave on the counter when she went to serve a customer. "A scarf. That will do. Any color. You choose it for me. Please."

They had gathered by now, Ginny was well aware, an interested audience. Two of Mrs. Sendall's girlfriends had come in and, while waiting for Eileen to serve them, were riffling through the dress racks in a desultory fashion, blue-rinsed heads the more ostentatiously turned away the nearer they managed to edge to the scene of the action. Eileen herself, caught up in displaying colored tights to a spoiled ten-year-old, flashed Ginny a glance of anguish at missing the only man to walk into the shop all morning. Even Mrs. Craig, emerging from the changing rooms with her customer, gave Ginny a conspiratorial nod.

Perhaps all this growing attention influenced her; but whatever the reason, she went on to serve the man more quickly than was strictly necessary, and he, in his turn, suddenly seemed to want to get the business over. He took the first scarf she suggested, paid her in cash, and, thanking her with a brief and strangely impersonal smile, left.

"Who frightened him off that time?" Eileen murmured, passing smoothly by.

Mrs. Sendall's friends turned their bright, curious faces to Ginny like two pecking birds. Gossip was their life, but on this occasion they had information to offer. They knew the young man. He had taken the bookshop in that street off the High Street, and his name was Charles Davis, or it might have been Bravis, only that didn't sound very like a name, did it, dear? Perhaps it was Travis. It was certainly Charles, or at least they thought it was, or could it have been the name of the man who had the bookshop before? The shop had been empty more than a month. The owner simply disappeared one day. Everyone who took it on went bust. That shop was always changing hands.

Ginny remembered the shop. Small, dark, hidden away from the main thoroughfare, it apparently never succeeded. It was one of those shops with a jinx on it. Every town has them, and not always on side streets. The businesses next to it flourish against all odds, but whatever trade is tried, however willing and hardworking, the owner or the tenant, hairdresser, bookie, florist, tobacconist, comes and goes in sad progressions until even the door itself looks too dispirited to open.

So poor Charles Davis-Bravis-Travis was doomed to lose his stake. Well, he looked too poetic to care much about money.

Ginny's lunchtime that day came at three o'clock. They took it in turns to have the more normal luncheon hours. Next time she would have the twelve-to-one break. Outside the shop the sunlight was brilliant. The town baked in it, shimmering spirals of heat rising from the streets. It would end in a storm, everyone predicted. "We shall have to pay for this," Mrs. Craig had said complacently, as if the heat wave were a sinful act in which they were jointly indulging.

Ginny had a coffee and a sandwich and then rang Mrs. Sendall to see how she and Ben were getting on. It was very hot in the call box, and she had, looking out at the breathless, empty street, a sudden longing for those summer days when Ben had still been a baby and she had been free to lie under the shade of the trees in the garden and watch him tumbling and tottering along the paths, pulling his wooden horse. They would hear the car drive in and then the whistle of greeting and the sound of his father's footsteps on the concrete path as he walked around from the garage, and Ben would go lurching to meet him, chuckling and laughing, arms held out to balance himself, the horse quite forgotten. . . .

She felt faint. The hand about to dial the number seemed detached from her, someone else's hand. She rubbed the fingers together and pressed them hard against the palm of the hand, forcing herself to feel the contact. The fingers were damp with sweat. In the mirror above the phone, her face looked white, and tendrils of hair were clinging to her forehead. She pushed open the door to let some air in. She didn't intend to faint. It was a useless sort of thing to do, and it would make her dress dirty.

People would have to come and pull her out of the box and give her cups of tea, and it would all be too difficult to cope with.

She dialed the number and then leaned against the door, keeping it open. As soon as she heard Mrs. Sendall's voice, she felt better.

"We've been out to get some ice cream," Mrs. Sendall said. "I'd have got some for you, but I didn't think it would last. What a day, isn't it? Hotter than ever. I've made Ben wear a hat. He's hating it."

"Oh, I'm glad you did that." Now she felt like crying. It was ridiculous.

"I wondered if you wanted me to buy anything while I'm out," she said. "I thought there might be something you needed."

"That's very nice of you, dear, but I don't think there's anything. I got some salmon for supper. I thought we'd have a treat. It always looks so cool with a lot of cucumber, don't you think? Do you want to speak to Ben?"

"I don't think so, thank you."

"I've sent him off with a basket to see if he can find any strawberries. There might be one or two surviving. I'll have a nice cool drink waiting for you. It must get very stuffy in that shop. You leave on the dot tonight. Don't let Mrs. Levison-Wrightly bully you into staying late to write up labels or anything.

Ginny smiled. "No, I won't. I'll be strong-minded."

"That's right, dear. See you soon."

Mrs. Sendall was an unlikely sort of lifeline for her to have found, Ginny thought, but that's what she was turning out to be.

That night she fell asleep quite early and woke up wishing she hadn't. She had had the dream again. The dream that even now could not fill in the details she had never remembered.

They were driving along the motorway. She had said to

him, "Shall I drive for a while? You must be tired." They had stopped for coffee. She had said it again. "Let me drive the next stage. You can sleep." In her dream she couldn't hear his reply. She had never been able to remember his reply. Her own words were the last thing she remembered. They told her she had kept repeating them over and over again. "Let me drive." They said he must have fallen asleep at the wheel. It would only have needed a second's loss of concentration. They had hit the supports of a bridge. The impact had come on the driver's side. She had been in the passenger seat. She was unhurt.

Ginny woke from the dream covered in sweat. She turned on her side and curled up, clutching the pillow to her, burying her face into it. She kept trying to remember his face. That was the worst thing, how quickly the memory of what he looked like was slipping from her. She lay curled in a ball, hugging the pillow, and waited for the first light.

"It will pass," she kept saying to herself. "It will pass."

The next morning, as she walked up the drive with Ben, a car passed them going toward the house, driven by a middle-aged man who nodded his head politely as he passed. Ginny had the impression she ought to know him. It was the sort of nod you give to people you have met before.

She forgot about him during the day. Nor did she associate him immediately with the state of mind in which she found Mrs. Sendall on her return. Her landlady seemed restless. Normally, in the evenings, with a gesture to her age, she rested. Ben, dispatched off to bed protesting that it was still light, would often be followed quite soon by Mrs. Sendall. She liked to read in bed, she said, with her feet up. Other evenings she watched television or sat talking to Ginny while Ginny worked on a dress. She would make a cup of tea and think up scandalous stories of her youth to make Ginny laugh. But this evening she could not sit still. Ginny heard her upstairs, walking about the empty rooms. When she asked if anything was the matter, she shook her head. "No, dear, nothing at all. It's the heat, that's all."

She wasn't going to worry Ginny about it, Mrs. Sendall was determined on that. Just when she was settling in. And there was nothing to worry about, anyway. It was a tiresome nuisance, that's all. She sighed and leaned her narrow little arms against the sill of her bedroom window. On so still a night, the shapes of the garden were etched black against the fading sky. The leaves of the trees looked as brittle as glass. And yet there was a softness in the air and a trail of mist rising from the cooling earth. Quiet as a ghost the cat slipped along the wall, bent on hunting. It was easy to see movement. It would be hard to see a watcher, standing in the black shade by the wall. The blurred shape that moved there, was that imagination? She was too tired to care. She got into bed and lay still, looking at the ceiling.

"It's foolish to worry," she told herself. "What can they do? It's my house, and if I don't want to sell it, that's the end of it. They're not after the public good, they're after money, and why should I be made miserable to make money for people like them?"

With her eyes closed she visualized the stretch of open land that was her territory as much as Alice's: the garden, the allotments, the church, broken and empty of worshipers. She thought of the big Victorian houses that used to stand along this road. She thought of the town with its curling High Street and its conglomeration of styles from the fifteenth-century market cross to the blank-faced supermarket. She felt a great wave of affection for it all. She didn't mind how it changed and grew and expanded if that's what it wanted to do, like the natural growth of a tree. But she was too old to change, too old to be uprooted and forcibly planted in an alien soil. She thought of Enid Watson, living miserably in a South Coast hotel on money that was worth less every year. She thought of her other neighbors' houses now destroyed and all the cold cement blocks with rattling windows and ill-made doors that were creeping over the rich black earth toward her like an army of devouring rats. Surrounding her, threatening her.

She opened her eyes again and lay awake, staring into the night. It was easy to be brave when you were young. It was easy to be brave in the sunlight. It was easier never to fight. It was easier, always, to give in.

✦ 2 ✦

THE FOLLOWING DAY GINNY called in at the estate agents to see how the sale of her house was progressing. She was talking to the girl at the counter when a man came from an inner office and asked her to go in. It was the man she had seen driving up to Mrs. Sendall's house the previous morning.

"I'm so sorry I didn't stop and have a word with you yesterday, Mrs. Benson," he said, drawing out a chair for Ginny to sit on. "I must confess I couldn't remember for the moment where we had met before. I had forgotten you were one of our clients."

He sat down behind his large oak desk and smiled at her. "Shocking, isn't it? Very bad business manners. I hope you'll forgive me."

He had a practiced professional suavity that was effective, Ginny recognized, even while you remained aware that it was merely one of the tools of his trade. Under his kindly glance, his courteous attention, you felt soothed, put at your ease, even vaguely flattered.

She had met him briefly, she remembered, when she

first went to see about putting her house up for sale. It had been no more than a passing introduction by the young man who had taken on her business. His name, she remembered, was Morgan.

"I came to see how things were going," she said.

"Let's see, shall we?" He picked up the phone and asked for the file on the house to be brought in.

There had been one offer which Mr. Morgan considered too low. "As you know, we usually fix a price in our minds, below the price advertised, to which we are prepared to advise our clients to go under certain circumstances. But this offer is below that price."

"And that's been the only one?"

"Yes."

"No one else is interested?"

"Not so far."

"I thought the summer was a good time to sell."

"So it is. Don't worry. This is only the first nibble. It's not a bad little property, quite well kept up. It's only been on the market a few weeks, isn't that so? It can take anything up to three months, you know, before we find a suitable buyer."

"As long as that."

"Longer sometimes. And your house has its disadvantages too, as well as its attractions. The broken guttering, that patch of damp on the kitchen wall"—he ran his finger down the notes in the file—"one or two other things. I know it was your home, Mrs. Benson, and you would probably never have left it but for the sad death of your husband; but buyers have no special feelings about the properties they see. To them it is simply an empty house in a rather out-of-the-way village. The London trains, you see. Difficult connections—" He waved his hand negligently, dismissing it seemed all hope of ever successfully arriving at the terminus.

"What about local people?" Ginny said. "Aren't they looking for houses, too?"

"Of course," he said. "But not so many as the commuters, and they are not prepared to pay so high a price. No, it's the people who must work in London but don't want to live there. They are the ones buying the property down here now. And so far they don't appear to be interested."

It was strange how the prospect of a sale, even of getting back no more than the original purchase price of the house, seemed to be fading away under Mr. Morgan's gentle flow of speech. If it had been only herself that was concerned, Ginny would have got rid of the house at the first opportunity, taking the low offer that Mr. Morgan so deprecated, merely to be done with it. But the money she would get for the house would be the biggest capital sum she was ever likely to possess. It was the only source she had of protecting Ben's future. The money was going to be for Ben, and she had to see it was the largest amount she could get.

She told Morgan so when he inquired, delicately, if there was any degree of urgency on her part in disposing of the house.

"I ask," he went on, putting his fingers together like a considering magistrate, "because I am, naturally—it being no business of mine—quite unaware of your present financial position. There was, I suppose, some insurance?"

"Yes," Ginny said. "There was some."

"But, of course, that was two years ago, and I've no doubt there have been many expenses to meet. Money doesn't go far these days, I'm well aware of that. It's a tragedy. You young widows are in the worst possible position. Mrs. Benson—" He paused, for once apparently hesitating over his words. "Please don't think me impertinent or interfering. What I'm about to say I say in the utmost good faith. Your house is worth a certain sum, whatever happens. If you are in any financial difficulty, I would be prepared to make you an advance against its sale."

"It's very kind of you—"

"No." He raised a hand. "No, don't say anything yet. Think about it. There would be no question of my being particularly generous or performing an act of charity or any rubbish of that sort. The house would be my security. There would never be any doubt that I would get back my loan."

"It's very kind of you, Mr. Morgan. Very kind indeed, but there's no need. I'm quite all right at present."

She was surprised and rather touched, particularly when, as if afraid he might have embarrassed her, he then changed the subject.

"You're staying with Mrs. Sendall, I gather?"

"Yes."

"Marvelous woman, don't you think? I've known her for years. And her husband, too. He was a charming man. I'm glad she's got company in that house. It's miles too big for her. Too much to cope with even by the Cissie Sendalls of this world. I've been trying to buy it from her for years, but she won't sell. Sentimental reasons, of course. You can't blame her."

"I didn't know," Ginny said.

"Oh, yes. That's what I went to see her about yesterday." He laughed. "My annual visit, I call it. Raise the price every year, and she's still not interested. Stubborn as a mule."

"Why are you so interested in buying it?" Ginny asked.

"The land, my dear girl. Have you any idea how much building land is worth these days? She's sitting on a gold mine, and so I keep telling her. Never mind, I can bide my time. One day she'll find the place is too much for her and want to retire a rich woman, and then she'll come to me."

"It's a beautiful garden," Ginny said. "It would be a pity to build over it."

"In a place that size," Mr. Morgan said, "you could put up six houses and still have roses around every door.

Still, it probably won't happen in my lifetime. She'll out-live us all." He laughed again and stood up, stretching his hand out for Ginny to take with a positively ambassa-dorial gesture of dismissal. "Good-bye, Mrs. Benson. I'm delighted we were able to have this little chat. And we'll see you get a good price for your house. Drop in any time. Always a pleasure to see you."

She left the agency in a slightly bemused state. She felt as if she had been entertained by a large and amiable cushion.

Halfway down the street a hand touched her arm, and an unfamiliar voice said, "Mrs. Benson?"

She turned. My day for being recognized, she thought. The man who had bought the birthday scarf for his niece didn't look quite so tall out of the shop. He looked more relaxed too, more self-assured. Different.

She said, "Mr. Travers," and then thought: That will prove to be the one name that isn't his.

"It's Travis, as a matter of fact," he said. "Robert Tra-vis."

Ginny said, "They got the Christian name quite wrong, but the surname was one of the ones they mentioned. I knew I'd pick the wrong one. I'm very bad about names."

He was puzzled. "Who are they?"

"You caused a stir in the shop," she said. "You were much discussed."

"Oh.'" He smiled. "A bull in a china shop."

"Not at all."

"That was what it felt like. I wanted to thank you for choosing the scarf. It was a great success."

"I'm so glad."

There was a pause. He hadn't quite overcome his diffi-dence. He said, "It's hot, isn't it? I couldn't stand my hair on my neck any longer. I've just had it cut."

So that was the difference. The tousled waves had been tamed. The effect was to make him look, in an odd way, both younger and more adult.

And that was why he had seemed to step out of the air. He must have come out of the barber's as she passed.

"I see you patronize my son's barber," she said. "He's good, isn't he?

"Your son?" He seemed astonished. "Well, yes, I suppose you could have a son. But I don't approve."

"You don't approve of children?"

"I don't approve of your having a husband in the first place."

"In that case you have no need to upset yourself. My husband is dead."

She thought there had been no need to put it like that. She could feel his distress and embarrassment. I'm being self-indulgent, she thought.

"Now you are angry with me," he said. "And quite right too. I apologize. Please forgive me."

He gave a great and theatrical sigh. "Everything I do goes wrong. I try to be light and flirtatious, and I end up trampling on someone's grief. The story of my life."

"Was that being flirtatious?" she asked.

"I'm not very good at it, am I?"

She became exasperated with him. "Don't be so sorry for yourself."

Unexpectedly he seized her hand. "I want you to have a drink with me. You've got time, haven't you? What are you doing loose from your chains? Is it your lunchtime?"

"Yes, but—"

"Don't refuse me," he said.

"All right," Ginny said. "I won't."

She drank gin because it was so long since she had been taken out for a drink she had become confused about her own tastes. She realized, when she began drinking it, that beer would have been a better choice on such a day. A long, cool beer. He saw her gazing at his pint and asked if she would like something else. She felt careless and drank beer on top of the gin. It had no effect other than soothing her. She began enjoying herself.

"I hear you're reopening that bookshop," she said.

He paused in the act of raising his glass. "Where did you hear that?"

"Oh, gossip has it. You know what it's like in a small town."

"Then gossip has it wrong. I haven't decided yet. I'm thinking about it."

"Do you know a lot about books?"

"Quite a lot. I've worked in bookshops. Would you like to see it?"

"The shop?"

"Yes. I was on my way there when I met you. They are offering the stock at a low price to be rid of it. I want to see if it would be worth taking."

She looked at her watch. "I've only got about fifteen minutes."

"It won't take long. I'll pick up the key from the agents."

The agents turned out to be Ginny's agents. She waited outside while he fetched the key. She didn't feel in the mood to nod at Mr. Morgan again, and by the time Robert Travis came out she had decided she would be back too late if she went with him.

"All right," he said. "You must come and see it another time. Tomorrow."

"It's Saturday tomorrow."

"You don't work on Saturdays?"

"Not tomorrow. It's my turn to have a free one."

"All the better," he said.

"No. I'm sorry. Not tomorrow."

He didn't argue. "Monday, then. I'll collect you from the shop."

"All right," Ginny said. "Thank you."

"I want your opinion," he said. "I've decided it's vital."

She smiled and left him. In spite of what he had said, he was very good at flirtations.

Ben lay flat in his hiding place among the seeding cabbages and willow herb and wondered whether it was time to go home for lunch. He had been down by the creek all morning, and he wasn't sure if Mrs. Sendall's whistle could be heard from as far away as that. He had a suspicion his mother and Mrs. Sendall wouldn't want him hanging around the creek. It was the sort of place adults warned you off. But no one had actually told him not to go there. "Don't go too far," Mrs. Sendall's morning admonition, wasn't the same as "Don't go as far as the creek."

He had only recently discovered it. Before then the empty church had been the limit of his exploration. It was boarded up with a big padlock and chain on the doors, but someone had pulled away a couple of planks from the small side entrance, leaving enough room to slip inside. You had to be careful not to get caught up on projecting nails and bits of rotting wood. The first time he had ripped the pocket of his shorts. Mrs. Sendall had stitched it up for him without even asking how it had happened. He didn't think she had told his mother because nothing had been said about it.

He always made a careful reconnoiter before going inside the church. With only one entrance it would be easy to be trapped. The enemy could put a watch on it and get you as you came out. He was careful coming out for that reason. He had developed a technique of sliding out sideways close to the ground. He had his special place inside, up in the right-hand gallery. There was a window there to keep watch from and two rows of pews provided cover for watching the door and anything going on below.

He had been at his lookout post by the cracked window when he had seen a man walking along a path beyond the church and had practiced his stalking in following him. He had been amazed at what he had found. A proper river, narrow enough to swim across, he guessed, though he hadn't tried it yet since he didn't swim well enough to do more than a few strokes before sinking. He was going to have a go at low tide soon. The banks were muddy and steep; above the tideline the sun had baked them into dry and crumbling ridges. Two derelict barges had been hauled up and left to crack and split on the scrubby grass. He had climbed in and given them a good going-over. The bottoms were black and smelly and full of interesting relics. He hadn't quite decided on their history, but he had several stories in his mind. He had carved his initials on them with his new penknife, and whenever he went past them now, he touched the initials with his hand, reasserting his ownership.

Farther on was a wooden wharf where boats could be moored. There were iron rings set in the wharf that weren't rusty at all so boats must still come there, though he hadn't seen any tied up yet. Next he came to a fenced-off patch of ground with the faded name of "F. Stone, Boatbuilder," painted on a board on the gate. He had climbed the gate and looked over the top. He saw a shed and another wharf and a lot of things spread on the grass, ropes and bits of wood and machinery. There was a boat on blocks and another small craft lying askew on the grass. A man had come out of the shed and begun to walk toward the boats with what looked like a chisel in his hand; but Ben's arms were aching, and he had had to let go and drop to the ground before the man got near enough for him to talk to. He was going to go and ask the man about the boats and how you built them and if he could sail in one another time.

On the far side of the creek there was nothing but a flat field. In the distance were houses and away to the left, the town. The other way, past the boatyard, was much more interesting. It led toward the big river and finally, he knew, to the sea. He had seen a boat with two sails up, sailing, and another coming up the creek with an engine going. The creek bent around in a big curve leading away from the town and into the open country, but it was a long way to the sea. He would need to make a proper expedition, with food, to get there and he hadn't organized Mrs. Sendall and his mother for long absences yet. He had to be back when his mother got home, or she got in an awful state. He really should have a watch to tell the time. If he could tell the time, he could time his journeys and plan everything beforehand, the way explorers did. As it was, he had to break off his investigations of the creek, as he had today, in case he was late back.

He decided, before he went home to lunch, to make a routine inspection of the church since he hadn't been in it for a couple of days. No one was about. He rose from the weeds and ran, bent over, dodging and weaving, up to the church.

The church had been built in a fine flurry of High Anglicanism, in the late Victorian era, to serve the estate of large and wealthy mansions of which Mrs. Sendall's house was a survivor. The houses were large because the families were large, consisting not only of parents and six or seven children, but aunts and cousins and other assorted relatives, visiting or resident, with the servants necessary to look after them. The church was therefore of a comparable size to accommodate the large and prosperous congregation who had subscribed to its erection and who regarded it as an extension of their own properties. They liked to have their own clergymen for their own use. The graceful Gothic church in the town and the various chapels that sat, squat but fruitful, in the side streets, were not for them, and as they had raised and sustained it, so their diminution and decline led to its own slow death. With a congregation, in its last year, of six, it was more than uneconomic, it was literally impossible, to keep the building up. The fabric decayed and could not be repaired. The wooden pillars that held up the galleries where the servants had been sent to pray were struck by the beetle; the plaster façade that had given a Palladian appearance to the red-brick shell fell away and could not be replaced. The ancient heating system collapsed, and shortly after so did two of the loyal six from resultant chills to the kidneys. The organ was removed to another, more fortunate church; the furniture, except for a few fixed pews in the gallery, was sold. It ceased to be a place of worship and became a place of no value other than the value of its building materials. The lead had long been stripped from it, but its bricks might be worth something when it was eventually demolished.

Ben walked around it, looking in a proprietorial way at the monumental plaques which remained on some of the walls and searching the cluttered floor for items of sufficient interest to go into his collection. He had found the church so far a rich mine of treasures, and he had only searched a quarter of it yet. That done, he went as he always did, up the wooden steps of the pulpit. The steps, guarded on one side by banisters only the bottom support of which, with its heavy round head, had survived intact, led into what was practically a little room, quite circular, and Ben had often sat there quietly, thinking about things. He counted the stairs in his head as he went up, and as he reached the last one and put his hand on the rail at the top, another hand came from within the pulpit and closed over his.

It was doubtful who was the more terrified, Ben or the man who had been at that moment in the act of levering himself up to his feet with the aid of the rail. Ben leaped in the air like Alice the cat when he pounced on her and was down the stairs and hidden behind one of the gallery pillars before he even realized he'd moved. His heart was thudding like a steam hammer.

"Where are you?" It was a cracked, trembling voice. "Oh, Gawd, oh, Gawd, don't say there weren't no one there. Don't say that, no, don't say that."

Ben peered around the pillar. A shaggy head attached to a thin scrawny neck had risen above the edge of the pulpit, and pale eyes so rimmed about and blurred with broken veins that they looked as pink as a rabbit's were blinking and staring about the church. They caught sight of Ben. Hands clutched at the rail, and the top half of a thin body encased, despite the heat, in a black overcoat turned green with age appeared in view. The man could not be very tall. Not much of him showed. He eyed Ben for a moment, then plunged from sight, reappearing grasping a bottle of wine. He took several gulps. Ben watched the Adam's apple leaping in the craggy throat, and fascination drove away fear. He stepped away from the pillar.

"Are you a tramp?" he asked.

The man pulled the bottle from his mouth and stared at him.

"A tramp, is it? Is that the sort of manners they teaches you at school, calling people tramps?"

"I'm sorry,'" Ben said politely. He came a few steps nearer and stared curiously up at the man. He had gray whiskers growing in tufts on his cheeks and long gray hair all over the place. He didn't seem to be wearing a shirt under the coat.

"What are you doing?" Ben said.

"What d'you think I'm doing? What's it look like I'm doing? I'm having a rest, aren't I? What are you doing, frightening the life out of people? Don't you know this is private property?"

"It's a church," Ben said.

"Go on, clear out. Get off out of it before I come and see you off."

"It's my church," Ben said.

The man swore at him. Ben knew they were swear-words, but there were a lot he had never heard before. The man said among other things that he would tear him limb for limb, cut his throat, disembowel him and so on. Ben knew what to do then. His mother had told him what to do if anyone threatened him when no grown-ups were about.

"I'm going to fetch a policeman," he said.

The man screamed at him. Rage distorted his face. Ben ran to the door. The man came after him, staggering down the pulpit stairs. He tripped over his coat and fell, rolling like a badly packed parcel onto the tile floor. The wine bottle smashed, and red wine ran in bloody rivulets around his head. He went on shouting. Ben ducked through the door and raced across the allotments. He climbed the wall at the end into Mrs. Sendall's garden and didn't stop till he was at the kitchen door. There he paused and made sure he still had his penknife and the bit of tarred rope and the piece of wire he had collected that morning down at the creek. He went into the kitchen as if he had just strolled up from the tennis court and sat down at the table.

"You're ten minutes late," Mrs. Sendall said. "Didn't you hear the whistle?"

"Puss, puss, puss," Ben said to the cat. She waved her tail contemptuously.

Mrs. Sendall smiled and shrugged and put his lunch plate down in front of him. Ben ate the food fast with his head down. He was thinking that if he said anything about the man in the church, they'd stop him going back there for sure and stop him going to the creek for definite certain sure. He wondered if the man had fallen down dead. "Kerplonk! Dead, dead, dead!" he said to Alice.

Mrs. Sendall poured herself a cup of coffee. She thought she might get the deck chair out and sit in the garden this afternoon. She would sit under the trees and have a nap in the shade. She ought to keep more of an eye on Ben.

"I went to see the agent about my house today," Ginny said.

"Yes, dear?"

"Mr. Morgan asked me into his office for a talk."

Mrs. Sendall was sitting in the chair by the window, knitting. She had gone over there to get the best light. She was making a Fair Isle sweater for Ben, and her lap

was full of different colored balls of wool. She had the
pattern spread over the arm of the chair and kept making
marks on it with the end of a knitting needle. She had
her reading glasses on, and when she looked at Ginny,
she pulled the glasses down on her nose and peered over
them.

"I didn't know you'd gone to Dent's to sell your house,"
she said.

"Well, they're the biggest agents locally," Ginny said.
"They seemed the natural people to go to."

Mrs. Sendall pushed the glasses back onto the bridge of
her nose and went on with her knitting. "Have they found
a buyer yet?" she asked.

"No, not yet." Ginny hesitated. "I had a long talk with
Mr. Morgan," she went on. "He seems quite a nice man,
if a bit overwhelming. I gathered he's the manager."

Mrs. Sendall counted stitches under her breath.

"Morgan is Dent's," she said. "There was a Mr. Dent
until quite recently, but now Morgan owns the business.
He bought him out."

"I see. That would explain things."

"What things?"

"The fact that he seemed to be in charge of everything.
He talked about you, by the way. He said he'd been trying
to buy this house for years, but you wouldn't sell. He says
you're sitting on a gold mine here, from the point of view
of land values."

Mrs. Sendall carefully made another mark on the pattern with her needle. "Mr. Morgan is not a nice man,
Ginny. He is rather an unpleasant person, in fact."

"He offered to advance me a loan on the sale of my
house in case I needed money. He seemed very fond of
you. He said he knew you well, and your husband."

Mrs. Sendall gave a sigh. She put her knitting down and
removed her glasses. "If he offered you money, he's got an
ulterior motive. I don't know what it would be, but if you

accepted the loan, it would become clear sooner or later."

"I didn't accept."

"Good."

"Has he been bothering you? I know he came here the other day. Was that why you seemed upset that night?"

"He does worry me," Mrs. Sendall admitted.

"But why?" Ginny asked. "If you don't want to sell him the house, you've only to say so. He can't do anything."

"Things happen. Pressure is put on people. Enid Watson owned the house next to this. She didn't want to sell either, but she began to feel unsafe. Admittedly she was rather a silly woman, apt to start imagining things when the idea had been planted in her head, but the idea was put into her head by someone that living alone in that house was dangerous. Morgan kept on at her, letters, phone calls, visits. Always very charming. At the same time, things got taken, the house entered, tramps appeared in the garden and came to the back door begging for money, threatening her."

"But couldn't that have been coincidence?" Ginny said. "After all, other people than Morgan could find out she was living alone and unprotected in an isolated house."

"Of course, my dear. You can't prove anything. But Enid gave up and sold out. And then he moved on to me. He never met my husband, by the way. And the only times he's met me were the two occasions he came to the house to see if I'd be ready to sell to him. Oh, I'd had a routine sort of letter soon after my husband died, asking, if I was considering leaving the house, could they act as agents and so on. I replied saying I'd no intention of leaving, and that was that. Then about six months after Enid Watson moved out, I had a first visit from Morgan and soon after that things began happening."

"You mean men breaking into the house, that sort of thing?"

"Nobody got into the house, as far as I know. I think

he knows that would be going too far. I'm not a frightened birdbrain like Enid. I'd bring the police in straight away. In fact, I did."

"Good heavens," Ginny said admiringly. "Did you really?"

"Well, there did seem to be a lot of odd men hanging about. I told the constable, and he patrolled the road for a while, and it stopped."

"It seems to be going to a lot of trouble to get hold of property," Ginny said.

Mrs. Sendall could tell that Ginny doubted her. Not about the tramps, but that Morgan had anything to do with them. It would seem far-fetched, she knew, when Mr. Morgan was such a pleasant man to speak to and so polite to everyone and so well known in the town. He was on the council, too, she remembered. A person of influence.

"Why should he need the place so urgently?" Ginny said.

"He says there is a great shortage of houses." Mrs. Sendall smiled gently. "He endeavored to make me feel I wasn't doing my duty as a citizen in not giving up my house, so he could build lots of little ones and make an enormous profit. Only I happened to have noticed that several of the flats in the last block he built aren't sold yet, so I wasn't taken in by that."

"I was going to say," Ginny remarked, "he gave me the impression nobody wants my house because no one is buying."

"There you are then," Mrs. Sendall said. "It's no good him trying to make me feel a selfish old bourgeois capitalist or what-have-you because I won't play."

She wondered whether she should tell Ginny that it had started again, that she had seen a man in the allotments, watching the house, hanging around as the men had done before. She decided, reluctantly, that it was her duty. She had to think of Ben, even if it meant Ginny going away. She told Ginny.

"How many times have you seen him?" Ginny asked.

"Twice so far," Mrs. Sendall said, "but that doesn't mean he hasn't been there more often."

"I would have thought the whole point would be for you to see him," Ginny said. "If the idea is to frighten you."

"Yes, I suppose that's true."

"Have you told the police?"

"No, not yet. The allotments are public ground, you see. The last time the men came up the drive. They were in the garden."

She was very calm, Ginny noticed. She didn't know whether to believe her or not. No, she was sure something had happened that first time or the police wouldn't have bothered to send someone to patrol the road, but couldn't this time be imagination? She couldn't really fit the bland Mr. Morgan into the role of a desperate villain.

"Don't forget you've got me here now," she said. "No one's going to frighten you with me here."

"You are a dear," Mrs. Sendall said. "I am going to miss you when you go."

"Who said anything about going?"

"I thought when you'd sold your house. . . ."

"Let's wait until I have," Ginny said. "We like it here too, you know."

When she went upstairs to say goodnight to Ben, Ginny asked him if he'd seen any strange men hanging around the allotments. Ben went stiff under the bed-clothes. He crossed the fingers of both hands in case he had to tell a direct lie.

"Why?" he said.

"Oh, Mrs. Sendall thought she saw someone hanging about. I just wondered if you had."

"She didn't say anything to me," Ben said.

"Well, never mind." Ginny bent to kiss him goodnight.
"Just tell me if you see any strangers. And if you do,
mind you keep away from them."

"Yes, Mum." He was willing to promise that all right.

If Ben hadn't seen them, Ginny thought, they didn't
exist. Ben saw everything.

At breakfast next day, Ben informed them that they
were going on a picnic.

"So that's what you wanted the map for," Mrs. Sendall
said.

"What map?" said Ginny.

"You're not working at the shop this morning, Mum,"
Ben said. "You said you weren't."

"No, I'm not dear, that's quite right. It's my Saturday
off. But what's a map got to do with it?"

"Ben asked me yesterday," Mrs. Sendall explained, "if
I had a map of this district, and I said I had, and I found
it and gave it to him, and now he wants to take off and
explore it. Simple deduction, Watson. Am I right, Ben?"

Ben nodded. He had never been so excited by anything
as he had been by the map. It showed everything. The
creek and the river and the sea and all the roads and everything. Someone had even written the numbers of the
buses on the back of the map.

"We can get a bus," he said. "And walk. We can get to
the river and even to the sea if we want. We can, can't
we, Mum?"

Ginny felt that all she really wanted to do was to take a
rug out into the garden and sleep for twenty-four hours.

"What time do the buses go?" she asked.

Ben gave a bloodcurdling yelp of delight and jumped
out of his chair. Ginny caught it before it crashed to the
floor.

"For heaven's sake, Ben, calm down. I haven't had my
breakfast yet." But he was off upstairs and packing his
explorer's kit by then.

"Well, really," Ginny passed a limp hand across her forehead. "I'm sorry about all this. But it'll get him out of your hair for a day."

"He's very good company," Mrs. Sendall said. "Particularly since half the time he's not here."

Ginny laughed. "A healthy walk is the last thing I could do with. No." She held up a hand as Mrs. Sendall began to offer to take her place. "No, I wouldn't dream of inflicting all that energy on you. You have a nice quiet day."

"Oh, come on!" Mrs. Sendall became brisk. "I'll pack you a basket. If I had some gin, I'd put it in for you."

"And if you did, I'd drink it."

Ginny and Ben caught a bus at the end of the road and got off it at a hamlet that consisted of two cottages and a pub. There was a bus timetable hung upon a post outside the pub, and with what she recognized as rare foresight, Ginny worked out the times of the buses home and wrote them down in the back of her address book. Then they opened a gate behind the back of one of the cottages and followed a narrow lane northward. After a while the hedges fell away, and the lane became a track; the cultivated fields gave way to pasture, untidy, hummocky. The soil was light brown like sand, poor in quality, rising and floating at the slightest breath of wind. The track was dried and cracked, and their feet stirred up small clouds of dust. There was a wind blowing toward them that smelled of the sea. In the pasture nearby, fat sea gulls stalked.

The track ended in a rising embankment. Ben ran up it. At the top he turned to shout to Ginny, jumping up and down.

"It's the river," he cried. "The river!"

His excitement was infectious. Ginny dropped the picnic basket and rushed at the embankment as if charging an enemy fortress. Her sandals slipped on the smooth glassy grass, and she laughed, clutching at the tussocks of coarse grass and the seeding dandelions. The stems broke, and the thick white juice of the dandelions smeared her palms. Ben stretched his hands out to her, his finger gripping and pulling, his hair falling over his forehead with the effort. Ginny gave a squeal as she slipped back and Ben began to tumble forward. He dug his heels in, getting more and more excited. "Come on, Mum!" And she was up and feeling she had climbed Everest, exhilarated with achievement and discovery.

The river was, in fact, stately. It was half the width again of the creek below the house, and it was torpid with the lack of rain. But the tides gave it movement, swelling and changing it hour by hour, stirring the mud and shifting its reedy edges. It moved with dignity, acknowledging its nearness to the sea.

"There's a boat. Look!" Ginny said. She pointed eastward, shading her eyes.

"That's the sea," Ben said. He spoke with a certain satisfied awe. "If I had a compass," he added, "I could tell you a great deal."

An overwhelming feeling of joy in the presence of all that space and emptiness, in the distant beckoning prospect of the sea, exploded inside him, impelling him forward so that he began running along the top of the embankment, arms outstretched, his palms facing outward so that the wind pressed against them. He let out a long yell as he ran, an elementary song of triumph.

Ginny watched him. She stood quite still and watched the small figure tearing wildly along the path. She felt a sense of release simply in watching him, as if he were carrying her tensions and grief with him and flinging them away from him into the careless air. She felt lighter and younger and impatient. She began to run, too, calling after him, his arms now flailing like windmills. He ran out of breath and stopped and heard her calling. He charged back at her, panting, breathless, giddy, and they collided together, laughing, whirled about by their own impetus, tossed and ruffled by the wind.

"We've forgotten the basket," Ginny said. "Let's go back and get it."

They walked back to fetch it. They were calm again. It was as if now the wild celebratory run was accomplished, it was possible to be calm, to walk, to look at nearer horizons than the rim of the sky. Ben scuffed his feet in the grasses and stared down into the gently moving water of the river, looking for fish.

They collected the picnic basket and then by unspoken consent walked back along the embankment the way they had just come, toward the sea.

Ginny thought of nothing in particular as they wandered along. She was conscious only of the change in herself and was grateful for it. The conflict between forgetting and remembering, between grieving and living, seemed to have temporarily resolved itself. For today it was in abeyance, and she looked no further than that. She talked when Ben spoke to her, and tried to answer all the questions he found to ask her about the river and its life, and was amused by him and content and almost happy.

After a while they found their way barred by a creek, too wide to jump across, that idled its way through a cluster of trees and straggling scrubland to join the river. The path along the embankment came to an abrupt end. They could see it beginning again on the opposite side of the tributary, but the only way to reach it was to follow the creek back until they came to a crossing place.

Ben's frustration was not mollified when Ginny showed him that the creek was marked on the map.

"They've made it too small to notice," he said. "What a rotten map!"

"Aren't you hungry?" Ginny said. "Let's find a place to eat."

She led the way down to level ground. In the shelter of

the embankment the sun seemed to strike down directly upon them. It was very quiet; there was a hum of insects and besides that only a vague half-heard reflection of sound from some distant road. The town and the few villages that sprawled along the seacoast seemed removed by more than a few miles; they seemed as remote as a foreign country. They had come into a patch of land that had been not so much forgotten as casually bypassed as being without interest or profit. The land was too vulnerable to flood, too far away from factory or resort for anyone to build on it, its soil to poor for any use but that of pasture. No roads ran through it, only rough tracks and pathways. As they moved away from the embankment, they came across dried cow pats in the fields, but the cows had long been moved to another part. The isolation suddenly struck at Ginny like a shuddering chord. The landscape looked dusty, unattractive, almost sinister in its loneliness. She and Ben in their bright summer clothes must stand out like a clarion call, vivid flags that called attention to themselves. She turned toward the creek and the shelter of its few trees.

There, in grass still long and green, they made their camp. That was how Ben thought of it, making camp. He would have liked them to have built a fire, but he could see there wasn't much point to that, except practice. There was nothing to cook, and it was too hot anyway, though the trees gave some shade. To Ginny it was a gentler, more companionable place altogether. She didn't feel so exposed there. The warm flow of air too light to call a breeze and the murmur of moving water soothed her, lulling her sense of apprehension.

They ate the boiled eggs and the tomatoes and the ham sandwiches and thick pieces of fruitcake and drank the lemonade and coffee Mrs. Sendall had provided. Ben had his penknife out and prodded the ground for worms. He thought about making a fishing rod from a long twig and string. He had some string in his pocket, but it was a barren place for twigs. He went instead to investigate the creek.

"Don't go too near the water," Ginny warned automatically. "You don't know how deep it is."

She glanced at her watch. She must remember how far they had to walk back to get the bus. She pulled her cardigan from the basket and put it under her head as a pillow. So pleasant to lie back on the grass and rest. So pleasant. She closed her eyes and slept.

It was the change in temperature that woke her. The breeze that had been so warmly caressing now touched her with a chilling sharpness. When she opened her eyes, the color of the light puzzled her. She sat up and saw a black mass of thundercloud stretched across the sky in such a way that it seemed to divide it symmetrically into two. The clear half that remained looked white, its color drained away. The bright sunlight was gone, and a strange yellow light filled the countryside.

She got to her feet and quickly packed the picnic basket, calling to Ben. When he didn't come in answer to his name, she went to look for him. She walked along the path for a little way, calling him, but there was no reply. There was no sign of him on the path ahead, nor was he visible on the embankment that guarded the river or on the flat open pastureland across which she could see for what seemed miles. He was nowhere in sight. He had vanished.

Ginny went back to her starting point and began to search methodically along the creek, turning away from the river and going inland. That was the direction he had been going when she had last seen him, so that was the logical and obvious place to start looking for him. He was all right, she told herself as she walked along. He had only gone exploring. Nothing had happened to him. Visions came into her mind of him lying drowned in a tangle of weeds. Or wandering too far, getting lost, getting frightened. She grew furious with him. A cold panic began to build up inside her.

She was walking faster and faster, and soon she began to run. The creek seemed to stretch away from her forever, winding and bending in a desultory way, getting no narrower. The bank was steep and overhung the water so that she could not easily see what lay immediately beneath. The ground she trod on was marshy. A long way ahead she could see a line of poplars. In the distance something moved along the horizon, a car traveling a minor road. It meant that help could be reached. She wouldn't think about that yet. To go looking for help meant to admit disaster. Nothing had happened. She repeated it like a talisman. "Nothing has happened."

She knew she should stop running. She knew she was no longer searching properly. She might already have missed him. He might be calling her, and she would not hear. But it took an effort of deliberate will to stop. In her terror and guilt standing still meant wasting time, and in that moment of time who knew what might happen? The storm was getting closer. The air was tense and electric and seemed hard to breathe. She looked back the way she had come. How far away the place where they had picnicked. Out of sight now. Suppose he had gone the other way, up to the river. Suppose he had gone back to the picnic place and found her gone. What would he think? What would he do?

She closed her eyes in anguish. She must decide. She would go on farther. He must have come this way. He would be trying to find a place to cross the creek. She turned and found a man watching her from the bank.

She didn't scream. She took an instinctive step backward. The man said nothing. He was wearing jeans and a check shirt. The shirt had grease on it. So had his hands, as if he had been working on a car. But there was no car for miles. She could see for miles, and she had not seen him. He had sprung out of the earth like a figure of death.

She could not ignore him, so she faced him.

"Have you seen a boy?" she asked. "I'm looking for my son, a boy of eight. He came this way.

At that moment she saw Ben. He had climbed up the bank a little farther down and was running to meet her. He seemed not in the least surprised to see her. Her appearance beside him at the moment when his latest game had begun to pall he took quite for granted. She flung her arms around him and hugged him. She wanted to hold onto him, to protect him, but he was wriggling to be free. She let him go.

"There's a storm coming," she said. "We've got to get back. Where have you been?" She thought she sounded calm and normal. She avoided looking at the man, but she was intensely aware of his presence.

"There's a boat down there." Ben was full of a delightful eagerness to share his adventures with her. "You can only see it from down there. It's his boat. It's stuck. The engine's broken down. I was going to help." He called to the man. "Have you mended it?"

Ginny didn't notice whether the man replied or not. A sudden wave of relief made her want to laugh. As soon as the man became identified with a boat, he became normal. All the threat and menace vanished. Even the air seemed to clear. He was a perfectly ordinary citizen going about his perfectly ordinary business. He had an identification; he had a purpose; he had a reason for being where he was which had no connection in the world with Ben and herself. He even looked normal now, as if he had relaxed, too. He must have been as surprised to see her as she had to see him. She must have seemed strange to him, rushing up and down the path like a madwoman. No wonder he had been so wary. No wonder he hadn't spoken.

Nor was there any mystery about his appearance. He had simply climbed up the bank from his boat. She had created the mystery, and the only threat in the situation had arisen from her own imagination. She was becoming as bad as Mrs. Sendall. She understood and sympathized with her now. How easily it could happen. One fear piling on another, and the commonplace became the dangerous; one alteration in light, and the natural became the supernatural, the stranger the enemy. Perhaps women on their own always felt threatened sooner or later. It was no one's responsibility to protect them and that made them conscious of their own vulnerability. They were the odd ones out. Perhaps it led you to behave oddly in the end.

She took Ben's hand firmly in hers.

"We've got a long way to go," she said. "I don't want to get drenched."

The rain caught them a hundred yards from the village. They had seen the sheet of rain advancing toward them across the fields and had run for it. The air was filled with noise. Ginny clutched Ben's hand more tightly. She was terrified of thunder and had an immovable conviction that to be caught in the open in a thunderstorm meant an inevitable death by lightning. If she hadn't looked in her address book and known that a bus was due, she would have been flinging them both to the ground at every jagged flash.

They ran for the shelter of the pub, splashing through muddy puddles. The bus was waiting, revving its engine. Ginny never expected buses to wait. It was a piece of fortune that rounded off the day, so that it ended as well as it had begun.

They arrived back at the house damp and happy, with the satisfied feeling of having surmounted enormous difficulties. Ben shouted for Mrs. Sendall as soon as they were inside the front door, clattering across the hall and into the living room. Ginny, following, saw him stop suddenly at the door. As she came up to him, she saw Mrs. Sendall seated in her usual chair. She was not alone. A man got to his feet as they entered and stood looking amiably at her.

He was slim and dark and gave the impression, odd in someone standing so perfectly still, that he would be light on his feet. A light man altogether.

"How glad I am you're back!" Mrs. Sendall exclaimed. "I've been thinking of you drowning in the storm. All that thunder and lightning," she said to Ben. "What a banging! Did you have a good time? You shall tell me all about it in a moment. But first I must introduce you to this gentleman." And then she said an unexpected thing. "Ginny, I'd like you to meet my nephew, James Aldous. He's going to stay with us for a while."

❧ 3 ❧

"I *didn't* even know you had a nephew."

"Didn't you, dear? No, I don't suppose you did."

"For some reason, I don't know why, I had the impression you didn't have any family."

"That's quite understandable."

"Not even a sister."

"Well, she's been dead for years," said Mrs. Sendall with what in any other person would have seemed callous unconcern, but in her merely seemed matter-of-fact.

They were washing up after dinner. Ginny was washing, and Mrs. Sendall was drying, and Ben was getting under their feet under the pretext of helping them. It was long past his bedtime, but everyone appeared to have forgotten that but him.

Ginny had tried to make Mrs. Sendall leave all the clearing up to her. She thought she would like to talk to her nephew, but Mrs. Sendall said that simply because a relative had descended on them, that was no reason for her to sit in a chair with her hands folded.

Ginny handed her the last of the plates.

"What does he do?"

"For a living, you mean?"

"Yes."

"Well, really, I'm not sure. Writes a bit, I believe."

"Honestly." Ginny smiled at her. "You don't know much. Aren't you curious?"

"We're not a very family kind of family," Mrs. Sendall said. "I haven't seen the boy for years."

"You weren't expecting him, were you?"

"No, it's quite a surprise visit."

"Why has he suddenly come here? Is he working here or something?"

Mrs. Sendall said vaguely, "Just a holiday." She gave the plate to Ben to put away.

"Don't drop it," said Ginny.

Ben was bored with the conversation. He changed the subject.

"Mrs. Sendall, what did your husband do?"

Mrs. Sendall's face lightened. She gave him all her attention.

"He was a professional mountain guide." She pronounced the words with great relish.

Ben hugged himself with delight. "Did he take people up mountains?"

"That's right."

"In all the snow and ice?"

"Perfectly correct."

"Did people fall down?"

"Frequently."

"And get smashed to little pieces, crunch, crunch?"

"Inevitably."

"You two ghouls," Ginny said.

"Did he take them up high mountains?"

"Exceedingly high ones, right through the clouds."

"Did they wear masks to breathe with?"

"All the time."

"Did he take them up Everest?"

"Don't be ridiculous, Ben," Mrs. Sendall said. "Whoever heard of conducted tours up Everest?"

Ben exploded with all the laughter he had been holding in. It burst out of him with the whoosh of compressed air. He bent over, holding his stomach and hooting.

"Oh, stop it," said Ginny. "He puts it on. Go to bed, you giddy goat."

"Giddy goat," said Ben. "Giddy goat!"

"You've set him off now," said Mrs. Sendall.

"Ben, stop it! You'll choke yourself. I don't know, I suppose it's overexcitement. All the amazing adventures of the day." He was spinning around the room, still hooting.

Mrs. Sendall was a believer in the amazing virtues of bribery.

"Do you want some cake before you go to bed, Ben?" she asked him calmly.

He spun to a stop and blinked at them. His eyes were full of tears of laughter.

"You're a mad creature," Ginny said affectionately. She put her arm around his waist. "I'll have some cake too," she said. "I've got the most enormous appetite tonight, I can't think why."

She sat at the kitchen table side by side with her son and munched fruitcake. She seemed to have discarded ten years in a single day. Mrs. Sendall had never seen her so free of care. The inner tension that had been so clearly reflected in the taut planes of her face and the heartbreaking sadness of her eyes seemed, for the moment anyway, to have dissolved away. She looked as round-faced and merry as a schoolgirl, and as young.

"What about your nephew?" Ginny said. "Aren't we neglecting him?"

"He's all right," Mrs. Sendall said. "He's unpacking. . . . Your walk did you good," she added, and thought how inadequate such remarks were.

"I'm going to sleep tonight," Ginny said and felt almost confident that she would.

Ginny was never quite sure when she began to distrust James Aldous, but it was probably as soon as the day after his arrival.

That day was a Sunday, and Mrs. Sendall had as usual gone to church. It was, she cheerfully asserted, a practice that was more a habit than anything else at this stage of her life, since she found it much easier to concentrate on religion at home saying her nightly prayers than during the service with its set pattern familiar almost to boredom and those disconcertingly intoned psalms that she had never been able to get on with. She used to read the words to herself and ignore the chanting which made nonsense of all the rhythms.

"I meet some of my contemporaries, though," she said. "And have the satisfaction of seeing how much more decrepit they are than I. The creaking of rheumaticky knees when the vicar calls us to prayer has to be heard to be believed."

James, rather to Ginny's surprise, accompanied his aunt.

"I'm only taking him to give the congregation the chance of seeing a handsome male of under forty."

James laughed. Mrs. Sendall patted his arm. She looked very spry that morning and was wearing a saucy straw hat beneath which her lively eyes shone with an adventurous light. "He's my guest, so he can't refuse my whims."

He was indeed, Ginny had to admit, a handsome man. He had a Celtic look, dark hair, light eyes, with a well-defined bone structure that gave both character and sensitivity to his face. He had been so far almost alarmingly unobtrusive. She had seen nothing of him the previous night since dinner, and at dinner he had somehow managed to efface himself so that although he left an impression of charm and good manners he had actually said very little. Mrs. Sendall and Ben had done most of the talking. The river, the picnic, the storm, the boat with the broken engine had been the topics, and once started on the recounting of his odyssey, it was practically impossible to stop Ben. James Aldous didn't try to stop him. If anything, unobtrusively, he encouraged him to go into every detail.

He had qualities of stillness, of self-possession and self-containment that reminded Ginny of Alice, the cat, padding along her mysterious ways with an elegant disdain of the rest of the world. James Aldous was elegant. He spoke in a pleasant, unaccented voice. He seemed fond of his aunt. He talked to Ben as an equal. He watched Ginny with interest and speculation.

His going to church could be hypocrisy or simple good manners. Did it really matter to her? Ginny yawned, lying back in her deck chair. Nearby, Alice lay in gently breathing abandonment to the sun. Earlier, Ginny had been idly making daisy chains, and Ben had wound them around the sleeping Alice's neck and ears so that she looked like a furry Primavera as she lay, adorned and decorated, in the long grass.

The storm had cleared the air without breaking the heat wave, but in some way it was a softer, more tolerable heat than that of the past week. Instead of the hard, unyielding arc of blue overhead, small clouds puffed their friendly way across the sky, and there was movement and change and a constant alteration of shadows and tones.

"My aunt tells me you work too hard. Is that why you have the look of a drowned mermaid?"

Ginny opened her eyes. At first she could see nothing because his figure blocked the sun; then he squatted on his heels beside her. She shaded her eyes.

"So you're back."

"Yes, we're back."

"Did you enjoy it?"

"Very much. They played some hymns I hadn't sung since my schooldays, so I had a good bellow."

"That must have livened things up."

"I believe it was appreciated. Where does that go?" He waved a negligent hand toward the end of the garden.

"Nowhere in particular. There are allotments beyond the garden."

"I thought there was a river."

"There's a creek at the bottom of the allotments, I believe. I haven't been down there yet. I don't think much goes on there." She looked at him curiously. "I thought you knew this place."

"I've never been here that I remember." He placed a light hand on Alice's stomach. She curled her paws up and stretched, with a series of luxurious tremors. "I suppose you know this cat's pregnant. What a delightful picture she makes. What relaxation. Why don't you copy her?"

"In what way exactly?"

"Relax. You're so tense. You're sitting on that deckchair as if it's made of steel spikes."

"You just said I looked like a drowned mermaid. There can't be anything more relaxed than that, surely. And how can mermaids drown, anyway?"

"They have to come up for air, like whales." He was sitting on the ground now, cross-legged, his wrists resting easily on his knees. "I hope it's not my company that's stiffening you up like this."

"I'm not stiff." She felt she was being provoked. "Have you seen Ben?" she said. "I don't want him wandering miles away when lunch is nearly ready."

He got to his feet in one lithe movement, like a dancer. "I'll go and find him."

She protested. "There's no need."

He smiled. "It's a pleasure."

She was definitely being provoked.

As soon as he had gone, she got up and went into the kitchen.

"How long is James staying?"

Mrs. Sendall was turning the roasting potatoes. "Why, dear, don't you like him?"

"I don't know what I think of him. I only wondered."

"It depends," Mrs. Sendall said vaguely. "That looks a nice shoulder of lamb, doesn't it?"

From the kitchen window Ginny could see James walking down the garden toward the tennis court. Then he moved out of view, and immediately the garden seemed oddly empty.

"He's like a magician," she said.

"What an extraordinary thing to say," Mrs. Sendall said. "What do you mean?"

"He gives the impression of knowing more than we do and having powers we have no access to."

Mrs. Sendall looked at her with respect. "How perceptive of you, Ginny. Yes, I suppose he does seem a bit like that. But he's very charming."

"Oh, yes," said Ginny. "He's certainly charming."

At twelve o'clock precisely the following day, Robert Travis came into the dress shop. Ginny and Mrs. Craig were behind the counter doing a bit of mild stocktaking. Eileen was in front of one of the long mirrors sticking back a straying set of false eyelashes. There were no customers. Monday was always a slow day.

Eileen saw Robert first, through the looking glass. She licked her fingers, gave a final delicate shove to the lashes, and, with a sly glance at Ginny, glided up to him.

"May I help you, sir?" She paused between the "you" and the "sir," opening her now rigidly lashed eyes very wide in the pause.

"Really," murmured Mrs. Craig. "She shouldn't make fun of the customers. It's not at all the thing."

"It's me she's teasing," Ginny said. "Not him." Over Eileen's shoulder, Robert was sending mute pleas for help.

"I'm sorry, Robert," Ginny said. "I'm not off till one."

He found his voice. "I thought twelve o'clock was your time."

"That was Friday. Lunch here is a movable feast."

"Aren't you going to buy anything?" Eileen said. "Mrs. Levison-Wrightly doesn't encourage the purely social visitor, you know."

"Eileen!" Mrs. Craig hissed. "Get on with your work."

Eileen flapped her hands. "Work, work! What work? What's a young girl like me doing indoors on a hot summer day like this?"

"Exactly what I was thinking about you," Robert said to Ginny.

"Why don't you go?" Eileen said. "There's nothing doing here."

"Oh, it's him, of course," Mrs. Craig cried suddenly. "Your friend." She didn't bother to lower her voice. She was too pleased to have got the situation sorted out. "Yes, why don't you go out now? I'll wait till you get back. I've nothing to buy at the shops today anyway."

"Cold meat on Mondays," said Eileen.

"You're too cheeky, young woman. You wait till you've a meal to get every day."

"When I do, it'll be a bit more interesting than chops three times a week and frozen cod steaks in between."

Ginny felt impelled to cry, "Now, now!" She picked up her handbag and, grasping Robert decisively by the elbow, steered him out of the shop into the street. It seemed the simplest thing to do.

"She's very lively," Robert remarked. Ginny thought Eileen would be pleased by this reaction.

"She's getting married in September," she said. "She ought to be lively." When Robert stopped short in a kind of anguished silence, she didn't grasp the reason for a few seconds, and when she did, she became quite cross.

"There's no need to watch my feelings to that extent," she remarked. "I'm not going to go into a decline because someone's getting a husband and I've lost one. I'm not that much of a self-pitying idiot."

He held his hands up. "I'm sorry, I'm sorry."

"And if you don't stop this awful habit of apologizing every five minutes, we part company. I can't stand it."

She thought the heat must have at last affected her, or the picnic on Saturday, or James Aldous' arrival, but whatever the cause, she seemed to have lost some kind of opaque layer between herself and the people around her that she hadn't even noticed was there, a muffling, dimming insensitivity to anything but her own affairs that had acted both as insulator and prison. Now she laughed more, she was sleeping better, and she snapped when irritated, like other people. It seemed a long time since anything had mattered enough to snap about.

"Look," Robert was saying. "I mean, how can one apologize for apologizing?"

She smiled. "Let me do it. I'm sorry. I shouldn't be so rude. Let's go to your bookshop and look at all your books."

He stopped again, and Ginny repressed an inward exasperation that she was, despite her previous outburst, still too polite to voice. She liked him, she liked him very much, but he did appear to suffer from an inability to conduct any conversation on the move, which was resulting in a greatly retarded progress down the street. They had left the shop minutes before and were still barely thirty yards away.

"You don't want to go to a bookshop," he said.

"You may not have realized it, but as a matter of fact,

I know quite a lot about books. My husband was a pub-
lisher's representative. He would have dealt with your
shop, now I think of it. It was in his area."

It was the first time she had talked about him so openly
for months. It was easier; it was definitely getting easier.
She could have gone on talking, but she was aware of
Robert's unease. It embarrassed him. He didn't know
what to say. She realized someone must have told him
about John. Morgan perhaps? He had known what his
job was.

"Besides," she added, "I thought on Friday you particularly invited me to see the shop."

"That was just an excuse to keep you with me," Robert
said. "I was too shy to tell you outright I wanted to see
you again."

"I don't know," Ginny remarked, looking him up and
down. "You don't look all that inexperienced with women
to me."

"How disappointing," he said. "I thought I did."

"And what about my opinion being vital as to whether
you took the shop or not?"

"Oh, it is!" he protested. "Absolutely vital. Let's dis-
cuss it over lunch."

They were standing beside a red MGB parked at the
curb. To Ginny's surprise, Robert bent down and opened
the door of this car.

"This is yours?"

"For the time being."

The dallying down the street was explained. She got in
and watched Robert as with casual competence he extri-
cated the car from its position between two others and
turned it onto the road out of the town.

"I thought we'd go out into the country," he said. "I
know a nice little pub."

At times, Ginny thought, he was too good to be true.
The trouble was he appeared to be playing two different
parts. It was as if he hadn't quite decided in his own mind

which role would prove to be the more effective with her and was trying them both out for size: the shy, tousled academic aimed to bring out the mother in her or the confident man of the world to sweep her off her widowed and presumably frustrated feet.

It was, however, flattering enough that a personable young man should care so much to attract her that he went to the trouble of playacting. And he would probably turn out to be an amalgam of both roles. It was, after all, possible to be shy and worldly at the same time.

He brought her back to the shop at two o'clock. She was windblown, fed, relaxed, and smiling. Mrs. Craig and Eileen watched her return from the window with an interest that might fairly have been called avid if it had not been so carefully disguised—Mrs. Craig by the excuse that she was worried because Ginny had overstayed her allotted hour for lunch and was risking the sack, Eileen by her loud concern for a job she normally disliked, rearranging the window display to include clothes that should have sold the previous week and Mrs. Levison-Wrightly was anxious to shift. Come Friday it all had to be done again. "Laying the bait for the Saturday spenders," as Eileen put it. She really had not, as Mrs. Craig so frequently observed, her heart in the rag trade.

"Did you have a nice time?" Mrs. Craig asked as Ginny came in.

"Yes, thank you."

"Where did you go?"

"She means what did you talk about," Eileen remarked, "and that means has he proposed yet."

"Well, really!"

"We talked about music," Ginny said. It happened to be true, so she didn't care who knew it. They had talked about music because he had discovered she was fond of it, and now she came to think of it, apart from the weather, the countryside, the pub, and what they were going to eat and drink at lunch, they had talked of very little else. The bookshop and his decision to take it or not to take it had rather been forgotten. It had been an enjoyable and amusing couple of hours, and she couldn't decide if the unexpectedly suave and knowledgeable Englishman who had entertained her was all a big act. It didn't matter because she didn't care. She had reached a plateau where enjoyment was possible, even love of a kind, the light, frivolous love that hurts no one, that lacks the capacity to tear one to pieces. She suspected that Robert himself had no deeper capacity or at least no deeper intention than that, which made it all square, or all fair in love and war as Mrs. Craig would undoubtedly have phrased it.

When she came out of the shop at five thirty, the red MGB was parked outside.

"I've come to drive you home," Robert announced.

"There's not the slightest need," Ginny said. She added hastily, because she did not want to hurt his feelings, "Not that I don't appreciate it."

"If you appreciate it so much," he replied, "hop in."

He refused to drop her at the gate and swept the car up the drive, parking outside the front door with a flourish of gravel and dust. As they got out, Ben came pelting up the garden, taut with curiosity. He hopped about the car, stiff-legged and tongue-tied with a sudden shyness in the face of such marvels.

Ginny, to help him, made an exceptionally formal introduction.

"How do you do?" Robert said politely. "Would you care to come for a spin?"

Ginny pulled a face at him, but Ben had catapulted himself into the passenger seat before the offer could possibly be withdrawn.

"Ben—" Ginny began.

"It's all right," Robert said. "I'll only go down the drive and back." He revved up inordinately loudly, swung around in a tight circle, and roared off down the drive,

Ben clutching the edges of his seat in an ecstasy of joy.

"Who's the beamish boy with the broken exhaust?"

Ginny, so absorbed with Ben, had not noticed James Aldous' approach. He came wandering up from the garden as Ben had done, and the cat, Ginny observed, like a familiar with its master, softly followed him. When he stopped, she curled herself gracefully and deliberately about his legs.

It disturbed Ginny to see such instant loyalty. "Alice has taken to you," she said.

"I happened to have volunteered to open her tin of cat food this evening," James said. "Cats are very fickle."

The sports car was returning. James asked again, "Who's the boyfriend?"

"Just a friend," Ginny said. "Just a friend." It was, she implied, none of his business, but he smiled at her then in such an unexpected, friendly way that she felt both mean and ill mannered.

"His name is Robert Travis," she said. "He's thinking of taking a bookshop in the town."

"I see. Thank you," he said. She wasn't sure which he was thanking her for—the information or her remembrance of her manners.

The brief ride in the MGB had the effect of reducing Ben to almost total silence for the rest of the evening. He sat in quiet and blissful reminiscence, nursing a glass of fizzy lemonade, while Robert was entertained by the adults with light conversation and gin. Ginny had been surprised to see the gin.

"James bought it as a treat," Mrs. Sendall whispered confidentially. "Isn't it nice to have a good stiff drink again? Ben, go and get some more ice, there's a dear."

Ben trotted obediently off to the kitchen.

"You've hypnotized him," Ginny said to Robert.

"I can give him a longer ride any time you like," he said. "I've never had such an appreciative passenger."

"Have you lived in Cranesmere long, Mr. Travis?" Mrs. Sendall inquired. "I'm sure I've seen you about the place."

"Very likely. I've been coming and going for the past month, I suppose."

"And are you planning to stay?"

"Possibly. I think so. I hope so." He glanced at Ginny. "That depends."

The glance was noted by them all, by James as well as by Mrs. Sendall.

"He's thinking of taking the bookshop that closed down," Ginny explained once more.

"Ah, then that'll be where I've seen you," Mrs. Sendall said. "Coming out of that bookshop. There's a very good baker down that street I quite often go to. I do hope you'll tidy up that shop if you take it. It got so frightfully dusty and broken-down-looking when that other poor man had it. And everything was always in such a mess inside you could never find anything you wanted. I stopped going there for that reason, and I think a lot of other people did, too."

"You see," Ginny said. "You'll only have to put the books neatly on shelves and you'll be a big success."

He already seemed to know the way to win over Mrs. Sendall. He praised the house and commended her refusal to sell. He would like to see over it all one day, the house and the garden. Mrs. Sendall was amused but pleased. She asked him to dine at some future date.

When he left, Ginny went to see him to the car.

"There's a concert at the Town Hall tomorrow night," he said. "Will you come?"

"What is it?" she asked.

"I don't know. Something to do with the local Music Society. A pianist, I think. I saw the poster from the car."

"If Mrs. Sendall isn't going out, I'd like to come."

"Go and ask her."

"Ring me in the morning, I'll tell you then."

He sighed. "Why can't you be more impulsive?"

Ginny laughed. "If you knew how I've been behaving lately, you wouldn't say that."

Inside the house, James was saying, "Is he a possibility?"

Mrs. Sendall looked at him thoughtfully without replying.

"She's very pretty," he said. "If that's what he's after, one can't blame him. What did her husband do?"

Mrs. Sendall told him.

"What a literary world I'm entering into," he said. "Publishers, booksellers. Do you know who owns the bookshop?"

"My dear boy, I haven't the least idea. Is it important?"

"Oh, yes," he said seriously. "I think so."

Emptying the ashtrays that night, Mrs. Sendall was struck by one of those mild coincidences that occur from time to time. One of her guests smoked the same make of cigarette as Ben. Among the others were the stubs of two expensive filter cigarettes, each about two inches long, each bearing a thin gold band about an inch down.

That it was no more than coincidence, she knew. Neither Robert nor James had met Ben at the time she had found the guilty cigarette end under his bed. Neither of them could be the source. However, if after this she found any more stubs in Ben's room, she would have a few words with him. Enough was enough in these matters. She made the resolution and then proceeded once more to forget all about it.

Ben had not been back to the church since the day the tramp frightened him away. He had a funny feeling that if he went back, he'd find him still there, exactly where he had left him, sprawled in a heap at the foot of the pulpit stairs; only it would be a lifeless heap, a dead, cold, and staring heap. It wasn't the thought of the tramp being dead that worried him so much as the fear that he might rise up, as had happened in certain books he'd read, a walking corpse, and advance across the floor toward him, fixing him with a terrible stare such as could drive strong men mad. Ben thought such a stare might easily drive him mad, too, and he skirted around the church very carefully nowadays on his way down to the creek.

The creek had become his favorite place; there were so many interesting things to observe and investigate, like Mr. Stone's boatyard, so it seemed both unfair and horrifyingly magical that, climbing up, as he always did, to look in passing into the derelict barges he had claimed as his own, he should meet that morning the frozen gaze of the dead eyes he had been at such pains to avoid.

The tramp lay in an odd twisted angle at the bottom of the second barge. His eyes were open. His ancient black coat was carefully buttoned. He had lost a boot. His expression was neither frightening nor frightened. He looked, if anything, slightly astonished. But the mere fact of his presence was enough to terrify Ben. It was as if the tramp had transported himself to this most private and personal hiding place deliberately to catch Ben out. "You made me trip," he was saying. "You made me fall downstairs and break my neck and you won't escape by steering clear of the church. I've followed you here. I can follow you anywhere."

Ben backed slowly away from the barge. Then he turned on his heel and began to run. He ran headlong for home with a blind instinct that would not let him look back for fear of seeing the thing pursuing him. He leaped up the cracked mud path and ran in a straight line across the allotments where so often he had dodged and weaved and laid false trails for his imaginary enemies. Now imagination and reality had merged, and he ran in a dreamlike trance. The dried and broken earth caught at his feet; the green expanse of weed and cabbage and limp, fading

runner beans stretched out before him like a vast uncon-
querable plain, a wilderness that could not be lingered in,
where the only chance of survival lay in speed. Far ahead,
the house waited. For a moment the sun, unnoticed,
touched the glass eyes of the binoculars that followed
Ben's progress from the distant windows. He reached the
boundary of the allotments. He crashed through the gate
in the back wall and flung himself into the safety of the
garden, surprising Alice, who was curled up asleep among
the fallen seedpods of the hollyhocks.

For once she was too lazy to struggle free. He hugged
her and clung to her and buried his face in her sweet-
scented fur. He had begun to shudder and tremble, and
he could not stop. She rippled her spine in protest, and he
rolled over and lay with his cheek against the earth, his
arm still heavily across her. It was warm. The sun beat
upon his back. His mind emptied. He slept.

When he opened his eyes, the episode seemed like
something he had dreamed, not real at all. Alice had ex-
tricated herself while he slept and sat drowsing a yard
away in a comfortable camel position, front paws tucked
inward beneath her fluffy breast. She gave a resigned sigh
when Ben picked her up and carried her cradled in his
arms down to the allotments and across to the church. He
was taking her with him in her capacity as a good-luck
object, a tabby cat not being as good as a black one but
better than no protection at all. She was far too heavy for
him to carry such a long way, but he persevered, arms
aching. At the church he pushed her ahead of him through
the gap in the boards. Her interest reawoke. She stood
looking about her, sniffing inquiringly. Ben entered the
empty nave and walked toward the pulpit. When he saw
that the heap on the floor was gone, he knew what he'd
seen in the barge must be real. He went back home. He
called Alice before he went, but she had found more
interesting paths to follow and would not come. The binoculars watched his journey homeward.

Ginny heard the news at the Town Hall concert. James Aldous told her. She was surprised to see him there. He had made no reference to the fact that he was coming when she had last seen him at the house. The concert was being given by a competent but uninspired pianist who was inclined to bang too hard in the Beethoven and retard too often in the Liszt. However, everyone appreciated the achievement of getting any kind of professional musician to come and perform for the sort of fee the Music Society could afford to pay, and every piece he played was received by the scattered audience with long and vigorous applause. Robert, Ginny noticed, was given to tapping his foot slightly to the rhythms. He must be very bored, she thought. That made it even kinder of him to bring her.

At the interval, he leaped to his feet. "Let's have a drink."

A modest bar had been constructed in the anteroom. As Robert plunged into the crowd surrounding it, James Aldous came quietly up to Ginny and handed her a gin and tonic.

"What on earth are you doing here?" she said.

"That's not a very friendly way to greet a benefactor. Drink your nice drink and be grateful."

"I'm with Robert Travis. He's getting me one."

"Live a little. Drink both. Besides," he said, "I've got some unpleasant news to tell you."

She gripped the glass tightly. "Ben—"

"Good heavens, I didn't know you were as nervous as that. No, not Ben. I'd have brought you a brandy if it had been Ben."

She put out a hand and touched the wood of a nearby chair. "Don't joke about bad news. I can't bear people to joke about things that can happen, that do happen."

He regarded her with a steady, serious gaze. "I'm sorry. I didn't mean to be offensive. They've found a dead body in a barge down by the creek. Some old wino."

She was relieved more than anything else. She had expected a worse disaster than an old man's death. She didn't see how it could affect her and Ben, and anything not directly relevant to themselves, she was ashamed to admit, was unimportant to her.

"What happened to him?" she asked.

"What happened to who?" Robert emerged victoriously from the melee. He looked annoyed to see the glass already in Ginny's hand. She finished the first drink quickly and put the glass down on a table. "Thank you very much, Robert," she said, accepting the second drink in a matter-of-fact way, as if there were nothing for him to be annoyed about. As there wasn't, she told herself. Anyone can get involved in these social dilemmas.

"James was telling me about a body they've found by the creek."

"An old tramp," James explained. "He was on wine spiked with meths apparently. Enough to kill anyone off. They think he climbed into the barge to sleep it off, lost his balance, and knocked himself out. He had a fractured skull. That, with or without the meths and the night's exposure, did for him."

"He must have fallen very hard," Ginny said. "I wouldn't have thought you could kill yourself in a barge."

"They're quite deep," Robert said, "and pretty solid."

"You know them, do you?" James asked.

"I know what barges are usually like," Robert replied. "I don't know the particular ones down at the creek. I don't go there very often."

"Ben spends a lot of time there," James said. He turned to Ginny. "That's why I mentioned this business to you. Thought you might like to be forewarned. It might upset him. Or you might want to keep him away from there."

"You haven't told him!"

"No, but children get to hear about things. Good-bye, enjoy the concert."

He slipped away through the crowd before Ginny realized he was going, before she had time to ask him any of the questions that had come into her mind. She wanted to know, for instance, how he knew Ben spent most of his time by the creek. And did Ben actually do so? Why hadn't she found that out herself? Why hadn't Mrs. Sendall told her? Was it safe? She began to worry about it at once even though she knew perfectly well that Ben was at that moment fast asleep in bed.

"My dear Mrs. Benson, what a pleasure to see you again. Are you enjoying the concert?" The bland voice of Mr. Morgan superimposed itself on the confusion inside Ginny's head like smoothly flowing honey. In his blue serge suit with the swelling stomach that looked as if it had been grown on purpose to support a mayoral chain, he had the air of a genial host doing the rounds, his glance already flickering beyond Ginny's shoulder toward the next port of call.

She murmured something appropriate.

"Delightful," he replied. "Delightful." She gathered he was referring to the pianist. "By the way, Mr. Travis," he continued, "is that your red sports car parked in the side lane? It's blocking an entrance. They're asking for it to be moved."

"Oh?" Robert was taken aback. "You mean I should go and move it now?"

"That was the general idea." Morgan smiled gently. "I'll look after Mrs. Benson while you're away. It will be my pleasure."

Robert, still looking vaguely bewildered, went, searching abstractedly for his car keys as he did.

The unworldly academic was foremost tonight, Ginny thought. She said, half to herself, "I can just see him in an unsuccessful bookshop."

"My dear Mrs. Benson," Morgan said, "not unsuccessful, I hope. He's an intellectual young man."

"But not businesslike, I would have thought. Do you think he's businesslike?"

Morgan did not immediately reply. Instead, he gave her the honor of his undeviating attention. In some way he did indeed manage to make it feel like an honor. Ginny was aware of the same flattering effect she had experienced in their interview in his office. She wondered if he was Welsh. The charm all in the voice and the manner and goodness knows what's going on inside the skull.

"I never met your husband," he said unexpectedly. "He was in the book trade, I hear."

"Yes."

"He visited the shop we were speaking of in the course of his business."

"Yes."

He paused. "So you know all about it? Perhaps as much as he did."

"The trade, you mean, or that shop?"

He smiled. "Now which do you suppose I mean?"

She didn't want to talk about it. She had been making conversation, and he was making it too personal. She should have gone with Robert. She was always so slow in her reactions. "I know the essential things," she said. It came out more loudly and more sharply than she had intended.

"Do you?" Morgan said. "You know, I'm surprised. Forgive me if I appear impertinent, but you give me the impression of having led a very sheltered life. You look so unworldly."

Ginny wasn't aware that she had revealed anything out of the ordinary in her reply. And what sort of answer could one make to that last remark? "No one can be sheltered from life?" "Cruel fate forces change?" The platitudinous possibilities were endless. She decided to change the subject to the sale of her house.

"Have you had a suitable offer yet, Mr. Morgan?" she said. "For the property?"

He laughed. "You mean to prove me wrong about being businesslike. You come straight to the point."

"I'm sorry. I know one shouldn't refer to business at social occasions."

"What better time?" he said. His hands waved in an expansive gesture. "What better time?" He considered her with those shrewd eyes. There was something not so affable in his examination. "I might buy the property myself," he said. "How much do you think it is worth?"

He was constantly confusing her.

"Haven't you fixed a price? I thought you had already valued it. Unless you want me to get another valuer?"

"No." He held up a white hand. "No need."

"But I must get a good price," Ginny went on. "As good as it is possible to get. It may seem mercenary, but I have to think of my son's future. It is my one chance to get a big sum together. But you must know this already." Hadn't they been through all this once, in his office?

He nodded. "I understand. And then you'll leave the neighborhood, I presume."

"I don't know," Ginny replied honestly. "I haven't made any plans yet. It depends."

"I thought your stay with Mrs. Sendall was purely temporary."

"Not necessarily."

This was clearly not the response he wished to hear. His manner cooled. "I wouldn't have thought it would be a very satisfactory permanent arrangement."

So you do want to get her out, and soon, she thought. She had a sudden wish to be unpleasant to him. "By the way, Mrs. Sendall was surprised to hear you had said that you knew her husband. To her knowledge you never met."

"She forgets. I played golf with him many times. We were members of the same club. Her memory is going, you know. Haven't you noticed? I've seen the changes in her since her husband died. Marvelous old lady, of course, but overimaginative." He granted her one of his smiles.

"I heard," Ginny said, "that the police came once because people were wandering into her garden. They didn't think that was imagination."

"You mean like the tramp they found today," he remarked. "Yes, a nasty business. It proves it's not good for you ladies to live unprotected as you do, in such an isolated place. Anyone can come drifting in. Any undesirable. And you have your small boy to think of."

"We're not unprotected at the moment," Ginny said. She could see Robert at the door. He waved to her.

"Ah, yes," Morgan said. "The young man. Mr. Aldous. He found the body, I hear. The police were surprised he spotted it. Couldn't see it from the path. You had to go up to the barge and look in it to see it. I wonder what made Mr. Aldous do that? He's an unusual sort of guest for Mrs. Sendall to take in. What's his line, do you know?"

"He's her nephew," Ginny said.

"Is he now? Well, he must be a very long-lost one. I've never heard of Cissie Sendall having a nephew. In fact, I'm pretty sure she was an only child. Well, Mr. Travis, all sorted out? Good-bye, Mrs. Benson." He took her hand. "I'll be in touch. I'm glad we had this little talk. I'm sure we understand each other better for it."

"What was all that about?" Robert said.

"I'll tell you later," Ginny said.

She looked around as they reentered the hall for the second half of the concert, but among the audience she could see no sign of either Morgan or James Aldous. Why had they come then? Just to talk to her? James with his warning about Ben. Morgan with his warning about James. Surely Morgan, who knew everything that happened in the town, would have known James was Mrs. Sendall's nephew. Or, she corrected herself, was calling himself Mrs. Sendall's nephew. But how could there be any doubt? Mrs. Sendall would know if she had a nephew or not. Wouldn't she? She sat in the dimmed light, with

Robert a patient figure by her side, and felt the first awareness of an approaching, unknown danger.

Ben was not asleep. He had been in bed for a long time, it was hours since Mrs. Sendall had told him not to read anymore and had switched off the light, but he was not asleep. He had tried to go to sleep. For the past hour he had tried almost desperately, but every time he closed his eyes he saw the tramp's dead face staring at him.

He got out of bed and padded across the floor in his bare feet to put the light on. Then he knelt down and pulled out a cardboard attaché case from underneath the bed. He smoothed out the coverlet and, opening the case, took out one by one the collection of his dearest treasures. Broken pieces of pottery and glass dug up from garden and allotment, the tiny bleached skull of a bird, six different birds' feathers, one rather chewed as though Alice had had a go at it, eight small pebbles, some acorns he had kept from last autumn. He arranged and rearranged all these things carefully on the bed, putting them in various lines and patterns. He liked to hold them, as well as look at them. None of the shapes and surfaces was the same. They were all satisfying and exciting in their own ways. But tonight they had lost their power to comfort. They didn't seem the same as before. Something was lacking. He gathered them up and put them back in the case and put the case back under the bed. He sat wearily on the edge of the bed, wondering what to do. His head ached, and his eyes ached, and he was thirsty. Listlessly, he picked up the matchbox from among the clutter on the bedside table and inspected the chrysalis within. It looked brown and dried and flaky. Shriveled up like a withered leaf. He knew it was never going to open. No beautiful butterfly was going to split that shell and unfold sticky wings in the sunlight. It was dead. It had been dead when he first picked it up from the grass. He knew that now.

He took it in his hand and went to the open window and threw it away from him as far as he could. For an instant, in the light streaming from the windows of the room beneath, he saw it floating down. Then it was gone. He strained to see it again, crouched by the window, staring into the night, and saw instead a shape moving down the garden toward the house. A primitive terror seized him. He had known he would come. He had followed him from the church to the creek: now he was following him into the house. He slammed the window and jumped into bed, curling up into a tight ball, the sheet pulled over his head. His hand felt beneath the pillow for his penknife. He clutched it to him and waited.

The slam of the window awoke Mrs. Sendall. She had been having a nap in front of the television set, quite unintended and badly organized since she woke up with a leg full of pins and needles. She rubbed it hard to get the circulation going. The television droned on, three self-satisfied gentlemen engaged in a political discussion. She switched it off and looked around, trying to recall what had awakened her. Something upstairs. Ben. She went upstairs to his room and opened the door. The light was on. Ben a nondescript hump beneath the covers. So he had been reading again after she had left him. She called his name loudly to see if he was awake. Ben had heard the door open. He almost sobbed with relief to hear Mrs. Sendall's voice. He put his nose over the bedclothes.

"So you're not asleep." She came into the room and sat on the bed. "There you are, you foolish fellow, you see what reading too long does for you. Overstimulates the brain and then you can't sleep." She smoothed the hair from his forehead. "You're hot. Don't you want the window open?"

He shook his head mutely.

"I do hope you're not sickening for something. Now you stay exactly where you are and I'll get you some

warm milk. I'll leave the light on, but it's bad for your
eyes, you know, having that bright light on all night.
Would you like a little one, by the bed? A night-light?"

He didn't say anything.

She went to the kitchen and heated some milk, putting
the kettle on for herself at the same time. She took a
night-light from the store cupboard, put it in a saucer,
and took it and the milk upstairs. She waited while Ben
sipped up all the milk; then she straightened the bedclothes and tucked him up. She didn't comment about the
penknife clasped in his hand, and she didn't take it away.
She lit the night-light and put it on the table beside the
bed; then she said good-night for the second time,
switched off the top light and went away.

Ben lay watching the shadows moving beyond the circle of light from the saucer, his eyes wide open so no one
would take him by surprise. But fifteen minutes later,
when the first soft footfalls approached the door, he was
fast asleep.

Mrs. Sendall had decided to have her tea in bed. She
put the teapot, milk jug, cup, and saucer on a tray and
carried it up to her bedroom. She took off her dress, put
on her dressing gown, and got herself comfortably settled
on top of the bed with her current novel and her tea. She
was on her second cup when she heard the creaking in the
corridor. It was very faint, like the lightest of feet touching momentarily on uneven board. Old houses do creak,
especially when the temperature changes after a hot day.
She went on reading, but her attention was only half on
the book. The sound came again. She put the book down
and listened intently. It came again, barely to be distin-
guished but once heard, unmistakable. Someone was
moving about the house. Ben? She put on her slippers and
went to see. In the dark bedroom, the night-light glowed,
spreading a gentle, diffused light. Ben lay on his back,
mouth open in the deep breathing of an exhausted sleep.

Everything was as she had left it. She closed the door and stood in the corridor, uncertain and a little frightened. Could it have been Alice? She was a big cat, Mrs. Sendall acknowledged, but those fat paws had never yet made enough noise to frighten old ladies out of their common sense. On the other hand, the cat could be wandering the house reconnoitering for a birthplace for her kittens. She heard the noise again, a definite sound from downstairs. She crept along the corridor and peered over the banisters.

"James! Oh, thank goodness."

He paused in the hall, looking up at her. "What is it?"

"Someone's in the house," she whispered.

"A burglar?"

"I don't know. I thought I heard something."

He came up the stairs to her. "Thought?"

"I did hear them. Feet. Walking about."

"Where?"

"Up here."

He went quickly down the corridor, looking in all the rooms. She waited, holding onto the banisters with her thin hands. Her ankles felt cold.

James came back. "There's no one here now."

She glanced up the stairs to the top floor. "Perhaps they went up there when they heard me coming out of my room."

"I'll look."

"Is it safe?" Her voice rose.

He went up the stairs two at a time. She heard him walking about the empty rooms. Then there was silence. She waited with growing apprehension. His voice made her jump, calling her from downstairs. She went down to the ground-floor hall to join him.

"There's no sign of anyone up there," he said. "I came back down the back stairs. Your burglar could have done the same and got out through an open window while we were upstairs."

"Yes, there are several windows open. I haven't locked up yet, with you and Ginny being out. Don't tell Ginny, will you?"

"All right."

She looked at him. "It's not imagination, James, all this. Believe me."

"It would be so much nicer if it were," he said. "Wouldn't it? For everyone's sake."

❧ 4 ❧

IT LOOKED DREARY. She hadn't thought it would be so
unattractive. Scrubby grass, weeds, dumped rubbish, abandoned hulks rusty and stinking—and the mud. Thick,
turgid mud, gray and wrinkled as an elephant's hide,
scattered with iron relics of bedsteads and bicycles,
dominated the dispirited channel of dark water that crept
down the center of the creek. She had forgotten it was
tidal. Low tide to match the low ebb of her own spirits.
She had had the worst kind of night. The dream and then
the insomnia. She had got up before dawn and watched
for it, and at the first pale easing of the night, she had left
the house and walked down to see where Ben spent his
time.

She found herself drawn toward the barges. Morgan
was wrong. You could see into them easily. Though not
unless you wanted to look into them. You could walk past
them and see nothing if you did not bother to look.
Would it all be spoiled for Ben now, all this unlikely
playground? Would he be afraid to come here again?
Should she let him? How lonely it was. Perhaps it was a

common haunt of tramps and derelicts. A little farther along was a boatyard. "F. Stone, Boatbuilder." There were signs of life visible through the half-open gate. Two men speaking, a shed door closing, a man approaching. "Hello," said Robert.

He looked astonished and then, as if he had remembered something about her, about her neuroticism, she supposed, her odd ways of behavior, understanding and wary. She understood the wariness. Last night, at the door of the house, he had kissed her. He had chosen the wrong moment, the wrong mood. She could not say to him: "Kiss me another time, not now." It was still too tentative, too fragile a relationship for that. She had tried, in excuse, to tell him about her fears, but they all dissolved as she struggled to describe them. There was nothing behind them. Imagination. Like Mrs. Sendall, she was becoming a prey to it and to memories and griefs and guilts she had thought were fading. She had turned her cheek against the soft touch of his lips and left him.

"You're up very early," Robert said.

"I couldn't sleep."

"Neither could I." He took her hand. "Your fault."

She moved away. "And Mr. Stone is very early at his boatbuilding. I'm surprised he still builds boats. It doesn't look very thriving here."

"You'd be surprised," Robert said. "Haven't you heard of the small boat revolution? Everyone wants to go to sea these days. It's the only way to get out of the traffic."

"Are you having a boat built?"

"I thought, since I was walking this way and saw him in there, I would see if he hired any out."

"And does he?"

His eyes were so watchful now, so careful. She felt whatever she did, whether she appeared to turn away from him or toward him, he would attach too much significance to it. If she smiled too directly, or if she was silent and withdrawn, he would be certain some strong emotion moved her, when it might be simple enjoyment of the weather that made her smile or an abstracted worry over laundry that made her frown. It would be almost impossible now not to plunge into something highly charged and intense. Acceptance or rejection, there would be no middle way. People should be more careful with their kisses, she thought.

"I've booked a small motorboat for this afternoon," Robert said. "I thought I might take Ben out, if you approved. Not far, just up the river for a picnic. I thought I'd ask Mrs. Sendall to come, too. Do you approve? Take the afternoon off and come too. Tell them you're ill."

"You're kind," she said. "That is very kind of you. Ben will love that. Are you asking Mrs. Sendall to make sure I approve? Do you think she'll come?"

"It will get her away from the house for a while. She'll be pleased to come. I'm almost sure of that. And of course, it is to make sure you approve. You don't think much of my capabilities. I know that."

"Oh, Robert." She could not help smiling. "You are always being so sorry for yourself. What were you doing, coming down to the creek, anyway?"

"Didn't you know," he said, "that it's a shortcut from the town to your house? I was going to walk up there and watch under your window. A lonely troubadour."

This time she really laughed. "I'm sorry. I can't take you seriously."

"I shall be mortally offended."

"Oh, don't be, don't be, sweet Robert."

"You should take care not to upset me. You never know, I might reveal my true nature."

"Well, that would be a change," Ginny said. "I think of you, you know, as a chameleon."

"Oh, I don't like to be a lizard. Couldn't I be a leopard, constantly changing his spots?"

"If you wish. Though leopards are dangerous—aren't

they?—not like lizards, and they never really change their spots at all."

"I should prefer it, all the same."

"And they are becoming, so I read, extinct."

"Not yet," Robert said. "Not quite yet."

James and Ben were in the kitchen when Ginny returned, eating breakfast in an atmosphere of comfortable masculine solidarity. They looked up from their papers as she entered with the air of clubmen confronting a non-member. Ben looked pale, and there were shadows under his eyes. She told him about the boat picnic. He did not seem as excited by the idea as she would have thought.

"Are you going, Mum?" he asked.

"No, love. I've got to work, you know."

"Are you?" It was directed at James.

"I don't believe I'm included in the invitation."

"I don't want to go," Ben said.

James folded his paper with a crisp rattle and laid it beside the marmalade pot. "The dead tramp has been removed from the barge by the police," he said bluntly.

Ben looked at him doubtfully.

"When?" he said at last.

"Yesterday."

"Did they take him in a box?"

"I wasn't there, but it would seem a suitable way to carry him."

"Where did they take him?"

"To the police station." It was clear to Ginny, James hadn't the slightest idea where they had taken him, but it seemed to satisfy Ben. He was still anxious on one point, however.

"Did they lock him in a cell?" he asked.

"For heaven's sake!" Ginny had had enough of the morbidity of this conversation. "What does it matter? Wherever he is, he's no longer down at the creek."

"No." Ben gave a solemn nod. "That's perfectly true.

He's gone from there. All right, I'd like to go on the picnic. Thank you."

"It was uncanny." Ginny related the story to Mrs. Sendall. "He started talking like an old man."

"He'll get over it. You must expect it. He didn't get to sleep for a long time last night. It's clearly been worrying him."

"James was taking such a risk, blurting it out like that," Ginny said. "Suppose Ben hadn't heard about the dead tramp. And how did he hear about him, anyway? I didn't tell him, neither did you, and last night James said he hadn't told him."

Mrs. Sendall shrugged. "Osmosis. Probably Alice told him. How are you, by the way? You don't look too bright this morning."

"I'm fine," Ginny said. "Marvelous. Mind you all have a good time. Don't fall in the water."

She didn't feel marvelous at all, and she felt progressively less so as the morning wore on. It was busy in the shop and airless. Some autumn stock arrived, and unpacking and checking heavy woolens and tweeds in the tiny stock room proved too much for her. Mrs. Levison-Wrightly, the owner of the shop, was in time to see her faint gracefully across the table.

She was sent home. Rather like a schoolgirl who faints in class, she felt, with a slight air of rebuke for not looking after herself better.

"You must try and get more rest," Mrs. Levison-Wrightly said, her sharp, sallow face severe. "We know you've had a trying time. You must try and get over it."

Ginny saw her job fading away from her. It would be a nuisance to get another, but she was used to it. However, for form's sake, she offered to stay. She protested she was quite recovered.

"Don't be silly." Mrs. Levison-Wrightly immediately

revealed the other side of her character and became kindly, almost sentimental. "My dear, I know. I've been widowed twice, you know. One year, two years—it takes
five years to recover. You never really do. Go home,
sleep. Get your strength back."

She walked home. The prospect of the empty house did
not displease her. As Mrs. Sendall had once remarked, it
was a friendly house to be alone in. Only the odd thing
was that this time it was not.

She noticed it as soon as she unlocked the front door.
She called Ben and Mrs. Sendall in case something had
prevented the picnic; but they had gone, and if James was
about the place, he did not reply.

She went to the kitchen and drank a glass of water.
There was some washing of Ben's she had left soaking by
the sink, and she finished it and took it outside and hung
it on the line. She was pleased when Alice came padding
out from the shrubbery and followed her back into the
house; she was glad to have the company. She could not
put her finger on what was wrong with the house. It simply felt different: tense, watchful, holding its breath, lacking the lazy, relaxed, expansive quality she had grown so
used to. Was it imagination? Lack of sleep? Or was she
really going a little mad? Had the fear that had driven her
to sell her house and come here been only too justified?
Well, she had no intention of sitting back and letting herself go mad. That was why she had run away. You
couldn't run away from yourself, but you could run away
from atmosphere. She refused to accept that she had
brought the atmosphere with her and had filled the house
with it.

"I need to sleep," she told Alice.

As if accepting this as the most sensible thing to do in
the circumstances, Alice followed her up the stairs. But
when Ginny paused at the floor where her bedroom was,
Alice continued up the next flight. After a moment's hesitation, Ginny, curious, went after her. The fat furry legs

and waving tail preceded her up the stairs to the next landing and along the corridor. Alice stopped outside one of the rooms. The door was slightly ajar. She pushed it open with her head and went inside. She walked across the floor to the window, jumped up onto the windowsill, and settled down, with the habit of old custom, to wash herself.

The room was one of those Mrs. Sendall had let in the days when she had the house full of paying guests. Like Ginny's room below it had a washbasin in the corner and a gas fire with a gas ring fitted into the grate. The bed had been left up, its bare mattress hidden by a coverlet. The carpet was worn and the curtains of winter weight, thick and heavy and a little shabby, but on the whole it was a pleasant room, well kept, well dusted.

The window must look out over the garden. Ginny walked over to it. On the windowsill beside Alice was a pair of binoculars. It seemed an odd thing to have left there. Ginny picked them up and looked through them. They needed only a little adjustment. In focus, the lichen-veined surface of the garden wall leaped toward her. They were expensive, powerful glasses. It seemed odder than ever for them to be carelessly left on the windowsill. And then she realized that they had been left for a purpose. Someone was coming up here regularly and watching from the window all the comings and goings in the garden. Alice knew about it. She must, in that friendly way of hers, have followed the watcher in here and sat beside them as they watched. It unnerved Ginny to think of it. It was harmless, of course, but it seemed so secretive to come up and gaze at everyone from an empty room, like a peeping Tom in reverse.

James' room was at the front of the house. He could not see the garden from it. Alice liked James.

Ginny sat down on the bed and tried to think, tried to analyze exactly what her discovery could mean, but after a while she gave up the struggle. Her mind refused to concentrate on such complicated ideas. She kicked her shoes off and lay back on the bed. It was like a disease, this desire to sleep. She seemed able to sleep only at the wrong times: on the picnic with Ben the day she thought she had lost him; now, when she really should get up and go downstairs, should persevere in thinking and making decisions. But it was peaceful and quiet in here. Alice had finished washing and, folded into a snug parcel, was purring herself to sleep. Ginny felt safe with Alice there.

The afternoon sun moved on, and the woman and the cat slept. The intruder came from his hiding place along the corridor and looked in at them. The woman looked beautiful as she slept, and as pale as death. Why not, he thought, let her remain that way, as still and silent as she was now? Two steps would take him to the gas fire. It was an opportunity that might not come again; why not take it? If she woke and saw him in the room, he could give a plausible reason for being there. He was a gambler; he had always been a gambler, seizing the passing opportunity had been his way to rise. But this was barely a gamble; this was almost a certainty. And so convenient, so desirable, so pathetic.

He took the two steps to the gas fire and turned it on. It hissed its serpentine warning, sibilant and sinister. He dared not move to block the window, and he could not lock the door. He must depend on other factors: the empty house, the long afternoon, the nearness of her head as she lay on the bed to the open mouth of the pipe. He could already begin to smell the gas. He stepped back into the corridor and gently closed the door. He did not push it to with any firmness in case the click of the engaging latch should sound too loud.

He went downstairs to Ginny's room and continued the search which her return had interrupted. Everything he touched he replaced with the utmost care. He found nothing, and he could not risk remaining in the house any

longer. He left quietly, and there was no one to see him
go.

Upstairs in the top-floor bedroom, Alice stirred from
sleep. Perched by the window, which from long years of
buffeting by gale and rain, did not fit as well as the door,
she had been fidgeted into wakefulness by the hiss of the
gas, by the irritation of the smell, and by her native instinct for survival. She shook herself finally awake and
jumped down to the carpet. Things were no better there.
She crossed to the door. It was shut. She considered it
with annoyance and pawed at the crack between door and
frame. She put her nose into the crack and worked her
head into it. The latch slipped. She inserted her paw once
more into the widened gap and pulled the door open far
enough for her plump, pregnant body to slip through,
wide enough for the gas to seep out into the hall, for the
fresh air to seep in and dilute the poison.

When Robert and Mrs. Sendall and Ben returned from
their picnic, the whole house smelled of gas, and Ginny
was still alive.

"I won't have a word said, not a breath, not a murmur,
about suicide." Mrs. Sendall, white-faced, looking almost
her age, placed her hands firmly on the table, leaving an
impression of a violently aggressive gesture.

"But, my dear, I never mentioned the word. I only
said"—Mrs. Levison-Wrightly paused, trying to remember exactly what she had said—"how sorry I was,
how pale and tired she had been lately, and then yesterday, the fainting—oh, dear." She stubbed her cigarette
out in the dregs of her coffee cup. "I should never have
let her go home on her own. How you must blame me!"

Mrs. Sendall sighed with exasperation. If she couldn't
get this one woman to accept it as an accident, how would
anyone? Already on her walk through the town to the
shop, she had become the recipient of the sidelong
glances, the hushed whispers. It would be so bad for Ben.

"She's all right?" Mrs. Levison-Wrightly inquired.

"The doctors says she'll be perfectly well in a day or so. I thought it better to tell you myself."

The other woman nodded. "And it was the cat, you said."

"That is all we can imagine. Ginny remembers the cat being there when she went to sleep. She was out in the garden when we got back. We think she must have seen a bird or something she wanted to chase and rushed out of the room, knocking the tap on as she went. The door was open. That helped Ginny, of course."

A sense of failure overwhelmed Mrs. Sendall. She felt as if she were carrying a great weight around inside her. She had so wanted to ease Ginny's life, to make her happier. Everyone knew it would have been impossible for the cat to have turned the gas on accidentally. No one had even considered the idea except Ginny.

"How is the boy?" Mrs. Levison-Wrightly half whispered the question, the way people speak of the bereaved.

"Ben's all right. Ginny wanted to come back to the shop today, but the doctor forbade it."

"Of course. Quite right. She mustn't come back till she's ready. Not until she's quite ready." Beneath her concern, Mrs. Levison-Wrightly was beginning to wonder whether she should start looking for a new assistant.

Ginny felt marvelously content. It was such luxury to be ordered to bed and forced to rest. The headache was going, and the sickness was past. She smiled comfortingly at Ben, who had come, small and worried, to her bedside. She hugged him and asked him about the picnic and made him forget her. They had driven to the boat in the red MGB, Ben squashed behind Robert and Mrs. Sendall, so that had been a second treat added to the first. The boat hadn't been at the boatyard but moored quite a way downstream with other small boats there to look at. He had steered the boat. Robert had said he was good. He went off, released from duty.

To Ginny's amazement, roses arrived from Mr. Morgan. James brought them up, all wrapped around with cellophane with a get-well note pinned to them.

"I wish I'd thought of that," he said.

The accident had emboldened Ginny. She felt in some odd way that there was no need for her to worry about herself anymore. She might have been gassed to death; but she hadn't been, and she was delighted to be still alive. "Let the dead bury their dead" meant something to her for the first time. You had to let the dead go or join them, and she didn't want to join them.

She looked at James, who had been in some degree responsible for it all by making Alice party to his garden watching.

"I found your binoculars up there," she said suddenly.

"Oh," he said.

"They are yours, aren't they?"

"As a matter of fact," he said, "they're Mrs. Sendall's. I borrowed them."

"Does she know?"

He did not reply.

"Why don't you call her your aunt?" Ginny asked. "She is your aunt, isn't she?"

"I'll leave you," he said. "You're supposed to be resting."

Half an hour later he was back, bearing a bowl of grapes glistening with the water in which they had been carefully washed.

"Robert Travis called. He left these for you. Ben and I washed them."

Ginny plucked several grapes from the stalk and ate them with enjoyment, putting the pips in the ashtray. "How cosseted I feel. Didn't Robert want to come up?"

"I wouldn't let him in. I told him you were sleeping."

Ginny laughed. James watched her with an air of wonder. "What an astonishing woman you are."

"Why?" Her cheeks were bulging with grapes. "Because I'm so greedy, or because I'm glad to be alive?"

"I'm very glad you're glad to be alive." It was the only hint he gave her of what everyone was thinking about the accident. It had never occurred to her that others might think of suicide. It did not even occur to her now.

When Mrs. Sendall came back, she asked James where Ben was. "He went wandering off down the garden," he said. "I didn't think it wise to leave the house."

"No, you were quite right. But now I'm here, would you go and find him? No need to bring him back. Just keep an eye on him."

Ben was sitting on the wall at the bottom of the garden, swinging his legs.

"I've been told to keep an eye on you," James said. "Got any ideas?"

"Shall we look at the boats?" Ben suggested.

"I don't see why not."

They made their way across the allotments to the creek. James noticed the detour Ben made to avoid passing close to the church. Once on the river path, Ben made straight for Stone's boatyard and nipped up the gate with ease to hang by his elbows, peering over the top. James found it simpler to open the gate and walk in. The yard looked deserted. There was a large shed with a padlock on it and one or two small craft propped up on wooden blocks. By the concrete jetty a powerful-looking motor vessel much crowded with nets and pots and fishing gear was tied up. A man appeared from below-deck and regarded James with a challenging aspect. James, becoming aware of a slight thudding along the ground, turned around to see Ben galloping across the patchy grass. He passed James and skidded to a stop by the jetty, staring with what to any owner would have been flattering admiration at the boat.

"Hello," he called to the man. "Did you get your engine mended all right?"

The man wiped his hands on a piece of rag and stepped ashore.

"You want something?" he asked James.

"Are you Mr. F. Stone?" James asked.

"No." He turned away.

"Is he about?"

"He's retired. I'm in charge now."

"You mean you're the owner?"

"That's right."

"Busy?"

"Fair enough."

"You hire boats out, I believe."

"Not as a rule."

"But you hired a motorboat out yesterday. This young man went in it."

The man glanced at Ben. "It was you, was it?"

Ben nodded.

"That was an exception for a friend."

"I see."

"I do fishing trips," the man said at last, reluctantly. "Take people out. Paying visitors. Is that what you wanted?"

"Maybe. Apart from that, do you build boats?"

He shook his head.

"Repair them?"

"I'm booked up. Got all I can handle. You'll have to go elsewhere."

"What about moorings? Any berths going here?"

"Come back in a year, mister. You're wasting my time now."

"Why a year? What's happening in a year?"

The man did not reply. He turned and went back to his

boat, disappearing out of sight. James jerked his head at Ben, and they left.

"He wasn't very communicative, was he?" James remarked.

"What's communicative?"

"Doesn't talk much."

"He didn't talk much before."

"When was before?"

"When Mum and I had a picnic. The day you came. We went on a bus. The man had the boat down a creek. You couldn't see it from the bank. He said the engine had broken down. But he didn't want me to help him. He didn't seem to remember me, did he?"

"Oh, I think he remembered you all right," James said.

Robert at last got Ginny on the phone. "Are you all right?" She had to listen to an outburst of cross concern. "You've got that watchdog guarding the door and answering the phone. I can't get at you."

Ginny laughed. "I don't know why he's been so protective. I told him he was overdoing it. I'm up now. I'm fine. I'm coming into town tomorrow for a while."

"I'll fetch you."

"No, don't. I don't know what time I'll be ready to leave."

It was a lame excuse, and the silence at the other end condemned her for it.

"Lets meet, though." She spoke overeagerly in an attempt at reparation. "At your bookshop. Why not? I'd like to see it after all."

"Not my bookshop. Yours," he said.

"Why do you say that?"

"Your husband's then."

There was another, long, silence.

"Robert?"

"Yes?"

"What's the matter?"

"Oh, God, nothing's the matter. All right. Let's meet there. When? Twelve. Will that do?"

"Yes. All right. Twelve."

She put down the phone, wishing with all her heart one could be insensitized to other people's feelings, like with hayfever or smallpox. She had enough trouble with her own.

She walked down in the end, letting the bus pass her. The avenues were lined with trees. The fat leaves rustled, too full of sap for autumn, too robbed of water for the freshest green of June. Warm, swelling maturity, in flower and leaf and people, began to seem to her the quality most to be desired, most free of pain.

She went to her bank first. The assistants looked at her as if she had come to make her will. "Could I see my statement?" she asked mildly, after cashing a check. She wanted to calculate how long she could last before having to take another job. She was certain Mrs. Levison-Wrightly was going to fire her. She knew the symptoms of old. She looked at her statement and called the girl back.

"There's been a mistake."

"I'm sorry. Are you sure?"

"Is it your computer going wild again? It's nice of him to do it in my favor, but it's not correct."

The girl took the sheet of figures away. She was not away for long. "It is quite correct, Mrs. Benson. The check was sent with instructions that it was to be paid into your account."

"But who is it from?"

"Dent's, the estate agent."

"Signed by Mr. Morgan?"

"I don't recall, but I should think so. Mr. Morgan is the usual signatory for Dent's."

Ginny nodded. "He owns it, I'm told."

"I believe so." The girl was polite and only moderately

curious. Ginny thanked her and left. She was surprised to find that she was boiling with rage. She swept into the office of the estate agent and was shattered when the girl behind the counter, at her first peremptory question, burst into tears.

"Good Lord, I didn't mean to upset you. I only said I wanted to see Mr. Morgan at once."

The girl took a handkerchief from her handbag and blew her nose noisily.

"What is it now?" Morgan came irritably into the room. He stopped short at the sight of Ginny, then spoke with a slightly lesser degree of harshness to the girl. "For heaven's sake, Doris, I apologize. I shouldn't have shouted. You weren't to know. Now for God's sake, stop bawling and make a cup of tea. I'm sure we could all do with one. I'm delighted to see you so well, Mrs. Benson." The transition from one gear to the next was incomparably smooth.

"I must thank you for the beautiful roses," Ginny said stiffly.

"Delighted, delighted. . . ." He took her elbow confidingly and guided her into the inner room. "Sit down, rest. You must rest after your ordeal. Such an unfortunate accident."

"Mr. Morgan, I came to ask why you had paid that sum of money into my account."

"Ah." He stopped speaking for a full thirty seconds, then clasped his hands together in a mannerism with which Ginny realized she was becoming familiar. It meant he was taking time to think before speaking.

"It's not enough?" he said at last.

"Well, no—it's, it's not businesslike," she finished helplessly. It was so difficult to be rude to someone who had not only sent you roses, but had paid a check for two thousand pounds into your account. Two thousand pounds was both too little and too much.

"I prefer," she said, "to do things the normal, businesslike way."

"Mmm." He rose and walked about the room. He sighed. He had obviously had a trying morning, and she was sorry to be adding to it.

"I was sorry, you understand," he said, "about your accident. Anxiety is a terrible thing."

"I don't understand," Ginny said. "Why should you be anxious about me?"

He smiled at that. "I was referring to yourself, Mrs. Benson. Though I am, of course, as you know, anxious about you. Do you wish to regard it as a first installment?"

"No," Ginny repeated. "I don't want to do it that way at all."

"Very well." The smile vanished. The mood became solemn, portentous. Ginny found herself sitting upright in anticipation of some pronouncement. "I am sorry we cannot arrange things in this friendly way. When I saw you in the office there just now, I had hoped—ah, well, it is your decision. I hope you won't regret it."

"But why should I?" Ginny heard her voice rising in the exasperation of bewilderment. "It can't be so difficult to sell. There must be people—"

"Ah!" He held up his hand. "But do you know them, how to find them?"

"I thought you would do that, as my agent."

"Isn't that what I've been trying to do?" He gazed at her and shook his head sadly. For some reason that annoyed her excessively. He was so damned patronizing.

"Perhaps I should go somewhere else."

"Your prerogative, my dear Mrs. Benson, your prerogative." He steered her to the door. The touch of his hand on her bare arm repelled her. No longer caring whether feelings were hurt or not, she removed the hand firmly and went through into the outer office.

"Let me know your decision," he called. And then he came after her, right to the street door, and said earnestly, "Do think again, my dear. You don't understand these things. You could"—he shook his head once more— "come an awful cropper."

She walked to the bookshop in a blind state of indignation, which was all the more irritating because it could be considered unjustifiable. Morgan had been highhanded and pushing, but it was impossible not to realize that he had meant well. He must have thought her desperate for money, and that was infuriating in itself. Nobody likes charity, especially those who could do with it.

She was, of course, miles too early for her meeting with Robert, but he, it seemed, was earlier still, for the padlock on the front door of the bookshop had been removed and the handle gave to her touch. She opened the door and went inside.

At first it was hard to see anything at all. Very little light came from the street, the small display window being curtained off by heavy green felt and the glass panels of the door so filthy that it was impossible to discern anything through them. The shop itself consisted of one long, narrow room divided into a series of connecting cells, somewhat like an elementary maze for scientifically inclined mice, by solid wooden bookshelves the height of a man. There was a smell of must and dust and decaying cloth. Somewhere in the back a dim light burned. Ginny made her way through the labyrinth to the lighted section at the end of the room where a large old-fashioned desk stood against the wall. Seated at the desk and apparently engaged in trying to force a drawer with a penknife was James Aldous.

"Hello," he said. "Has Morgan sent you?"

It was an extraordinary question and typical of him. He looked quite at his ease, tilting his chair back and regarding her with that amiable expression which was in its way quite as bland and unrevealing as Morgan's.

"I think there's a law against what you're doing," Ginny said. "And how did you know I've just come from Morgan's?"

He folded up the penknife and put it in his pocket. "Well, you do seem rather chummy with him, and I am expecting someone to come, breathing heavily and demanding my departure. I thought it might be you. Not," he added hastily, "that I'm implying you are breathing heavily. Not the best phrase to use in the recent circumstances. How are you feeling? Shouldn't you sit down? You still look as pale as a ghost. When are we going to see you tanned and healthy? It is the height of summer, after all. You ought to be out in the fresh air, not hanging around bookshops."

Ginny sighed and brushed the hair from her forehead with what felt a limp and helpless hand. In the space of two minutes he had managed to confuse her as effectively as ever. If Morgan was difficult, dealing with James Aldous was like handling quicksilver. She began speaking slowly, explaining things not so much to him but to herself, to keep events clear in her own mind.

"I came here to meet Robert Travis," she said. "And I have come from Morgan, though my visit had nothing to do with you or this bookshop. Morgan is selling my house for me. I'm not chummy with him. I don't like him, but he's one of the people I'm finding it increasingly difficult to avoid. I don't know what he's up to, and I don't know what you're up to either. What are you doing here?"

"Snooping," James said. He smiled, and she felt half inclined to throw something at him for the open boyish charm of it. Something in her expression must have conveyed this to James, for he suddenly got up and pulled a chair forward for her in a different, serious manner.

"Here you are." He dusted it carefully with his handkerchief. "Do sit down. I expect Robert Travis will be along any minute, angrily demanding to know what I'm doing with the key to his shop. But until then we can talk.

I came here out of curiosity, but most of the interesting things I've learned I got from the girl in Morgan's office."

"Oh," Ginny said. "So that was why she was crying. What did you do to her?"

"Do to her?" He was indignant. "I didn't do anything to her. If she was crying, it must be Morgan's doing." He paused. "And that's interesting he should get worked up over such a trivial matter as letting a client have the key to view a shop already taken, especially when it's not taken."

"What do you mean?" Ginny said.

"Well, your friend Robert hasn't committed himself as far as Morgan's office is concerned. He's signed no lease. Nor, apparently, did the man who had it before him, Charles Mayhew, the one who went bust and left all this mess behind him. He may have gone broke, but it wasn't the rent of this shop that did it because as far as the girl knows, he signed no lease either, nor are there any records of rent being paid in the whole time he had the place."

"I thought he'd bought it."

"Oh, no. And that's another interesting thing. Do you know who owns this shop? Dent's, which means, in fact, Mr. Morgan himself. I asked the girl what rent was being asked for the shop, and she couldn't tell me. There's nothing on paper about that either. It's all a very casual business. It must be a personal arrangement between Travis and Morgan. It hasn't been advertised or a notice of it sent out to people on their mailing list or even put on their card index. All there was was the key to the front door, which she kindly and in all good faith, poor kid, let me have in order to look over the property."

"Perhaps it's something to do with the previous tenant, Mayhew you called him, being in legal difficulties. Perhaps it can't be officially let till that's sorted out."

"There don't seem to be any legal difficulties. All the girl knew is that one day Mr. Mayhew had vanished, the shop was padlocked and the key in the office. Morgan told them Mayhew had had to close down his business, and that was all that was ever said. No one went into detail."

Ginny stood up. She had the oddest sensation of something shifting, slipping, in her mind. She began to walk along the shelves of books, trailing her fingers across them.

"Junk," she said suddenly. "He said it wasn't a bookshop, it was a junkshop. As if he'd bought the stock by the yard, from street barrows, to fill the shelves."

"Who said that?" James asked. "Robert Travis?"

"No," Ginny said. "My husband." She paused, looking back at James. "It's strange—isn't it?—that I should remember that now. It's being here, I suppose, in the shop and hearing the name of the man who had it. Mayhew. That's right; that's the name. And John didn't come here for his firm, not after the first time, when he realized it was all secondhand stuff. It was for his own library, his own collection. He specialized in Victorian first editions. He came here several times just in case Mayhew had some treasure buried away in these shelves. He told me Mayhew knew nothing about books. That was not long before the accident. I'd forgotten. . . ."

She became aware of James' arm around her shoulder. She looked into his face, puzzled.

"You looked as if you were about to faint," he said. "You were swaying."

"I'm all right," she said. "It's just . . . things . . . coming back. It's weird. Things about him. Things he said. Coming back."

"He was killed in a car crash, wasn't he? Where was that? Near here?"

"No, it wasn't here. It was on the M-1. We were driving up north, in a hurry, to see John's father. He'd been taken ill. Heart attack. They thought he wouldn't survive. But he did. It was John who died."

"I'm very sorry," James said.

She gave him a half-smile. "It's all right. I can talk about it now and about him. I couldn't for a long time."

"Was Ben in the car?"

"No. I had had to leave him in the care of a neighbor. His name is really John, too, you know. Ben's a nickname. His father was called Ben, too, when he was a boy."

"Why that particular nickname?"

"Oh, you know. John Benson. Ben Jonson."

"Very literary," James remarked. "What happened to your husband's library?"

"I sent all John's books to his father. I didn't want them."

"You sold everything up?"

"When we came to Mrs. Sendall's, yes."

"And the car?"

"It was too badly smashed."

"Did they say what had caused the accident?"

"They think he fell asleep. I don't remember exactly what happened. They said that was usual."

"So I've heard."

"He'd had a long day. He should have stopped to sleep. I should have made him, but of course he wouldn't." She turned away from him and paused. He watched her, leaning against the tall shelves, not speaking.

"He had been worrying about something," she said at last, "before he got the news of his father. I don't know what it was."

"Something to do with Mayhew?"

She stared at him. "I don't think so. Why should it have been?"

He shook his head. "I don't know. It's such a funny setup. A bookshop, run by a man who knows nothing about books and who, as far as we can gather, pays no rent, and then suddenly vanishes, leaving all his stock."

"Do you think something's happened to him? Something connected with Morgan?"

"Everything in this town seems connected with Morgan," James said.

"James," Ginny said seriously, "what are you really doing in this town?"

"Ginny! Are you there? Ginny? Is Aldous there?" It was Robert's voice, bellowing from the front of the shop.

James smiled at her. "The cavalry have arrived."

He made a graceful retreat. He pressed the key into Robert's hand, assuring him that having seen the shop, he was no longer interested in taking it, but that even if he had, he would have given way to Robert's prior claim.

"By the way, what rent are they charging you?" he asked.

"Nominal," Robert said. "As far as I understand it, they're only too glad to think someone may be interested in using the place and keeping it aired."

"Perhaps they are making you responsible for repairs?"

"No."

"Funny way for Morgan to do business," James said. "Wouldn't you think so?"

"Are you really going to take it?" Ginny asked Robert later. "It does seem, after what James found out, a funny setup. And the stock's worth nothing."

"I don't know what I'm going to do," Robert said. "I've got to go to London tomorrow, Ginny. I'll think about it all again. But there's no reason why one man should fail in a business simply because the previous one did."

"You're quite right, of course."

"I don't want to leave this town now." He took her hand. "You know why, don't you?"

Ginny sighed. "I don't know anything. I don't know why I get worried and apprehensive either, suddenly, for no reason, like now. Nothing has happened except that stupid accident with the gas, but I feel sometimes—well, I can't quite describe it, but as if something dangerous is creeping up behind us. Like that children's game, statues, when all the others try and reach you without you seeing them move. One moment they are far away, and then you turn and they are nearer, and then nearer and then at your back, as still as statues, but at your back, and you know the next time you turn away one of them will get you. You have to wait, feeling so vulnerable, unable to prevent it, waiting for that hand on your back. It's a very silent game. And this is like it. Nothing is happening, and yet you sense that everything is happening." She gazed at him. "Do you know what I mean?"

He was looking down, frowning. "And you don't know what is happening?"

"No, I can't imagine."

"Perhaps it's Aldous," he said. "Perhaps he's the one. When I'm in London, I'll see if I can find anything out about him."

"Robert, do take care."

"You take care," he said. "You're the one who must take care, Ginny. Remember that. And whatever you do, don't stay in the house alone."

✤ 5 ✤

THE NEXT morning Ginny decided she would go back to work. She got up and got ready in a determined frame of mind and was informing Mrs. Sendall of her decision over the breakfast table when Ben came hurtling in.

"James has got a car! Come and see. Come on!"

There was a sound of a door slamming and footsteps on the gravel, and Ben rushed out again. Ginny turned to Mrs. Sendall inquiringly. "He's not bought one, has he?"

"I believe he's hired one. He told me he was going to. He's off somewhere today."

"Let's have a look. Maybe he'll give me a lift into work."

They wandered into the hall and out the front door unsuspectingly, Ginny still holding the piece of buttered toast she had been eating. Mrs. Sendall, at least, was totally unprepared for her reaction. The car, which James and Ben were inspecting with masculine gravity and thoroughness, was a perfectly ordinary white saloon car with nothing odd about it that she could see; but Ginny stood frozen, the toast stuck in her hand as stiff as a piece of wood, her face aghast.

Ben noticed her. "Look, Mum, it's just like ours, isn't it?"

And then, as Mrs. Sendall explained to James in the kitchen ten minutes later, she understood. "Oh, James, how on earth did you manage to pick an identical model to the one Ginny and her husband crashed in!"

He rubbed his forehead. "I don't know. I'm terribly sorry. It's a very common make. I suppose the garage is the agent for them. They don't hire out any other kind."

"But the same color and everything!"

"I know. It's bad luck. I'm very sorry I upset her. Where is she?"

"Oh, she's about, pretending nothing's happened. She's worried Ben will notice she's upset, I can tell that. Oh, dear, on top of that other business—" She gazed up at him. "You'll have to take her with you. That's it. That's the only answer. As soon as she sits in the car, she'll know the difference. It won't feel like the same car. You can always tell. Then it won't worry her anymore. But if she spends all day thinking about it—"

James was doubtful. Mrs. Sendall was too concerned about another attempt at suicide to be put off.

"All right," he said at last. "If you say so. I'm not convinced amateur psychology is a good idea, but I'll take her, if she'll come. How are you going to make her get in the car, that's the question?"

"I'll bully her," Mrs. Sendall replied. "I'll make her go with you, and I'll keep Ben away till you've gone."

"I don't think she likes me very much," James said. "She certainly doesn't trust me."

"What's that got to do with it?" Mrs. Sendall said. "This is an emergency. It makes no difference whether she likes you or not.

Ginny, coming downstairs with a cold and resolute heart, found herself engulfed in a whirlwind of talk. She was not to go to work, the doctor wouldn't hear of it, and neither would Mrs. Sendall. She was to have fresh air, a ride in the country. It was no use protesting, everyone's mind was made up, she looked terrible, and Mrs. Sendall wasn't going to have her on her conscience. She hadn't recovered from the accident with the gas, that was quite clear, and the doctor had only said on the phone last night, and here was James, and here was the car, and not to worry about Ben, she had plenty to keep him occupied—

"But you didn't hire this car to take me for a ride," Ginny said to James.

"No," he admitted, "not specifically." He turned the car out of the drive and into the road. "But I'm very glad you've decided to come."

"Decided!" Ginny exclaimed and laughed. James laughed, too, and that was all the reference they made to Mrs. Sendall's high-handedness.

It was not the only reference to the car, however, for James could not ignore the tension that enveloped the woman at his side when he reached the open stretch of motorway and put his foot down on the accelerator.

At the first opportunity he pulled the car up by the side of the road and switched off the engine. Ginny looked at him in surprise. "Is something the matter?"

"You know very well what's the matter," James said. "You've been sitting there with your fists clenched and your face as taut as a drum, and it's putting me off my driving. Look, I'm sorry about the car. I didn't know when I got it that it would bring back horrific memories. As far as I'm concerned, it's simply a car I hired to take me somewhere I want to go, and I don't want to spend all day getting there. I intend to drive moderately fast, but if you go on sitting there sending out all these powerful vibrations, we'll both end in the ditch. Now, talk about it, scream about it, cry, yell, do what you like, but don't sit and suffer in that terrible silence. OK?"

There was a long pause. "OK," Ginny said. He looked at her carefully, then nodded and started the engine.

"It's not exactly the same as our car," Ginny said.

"Good."

"We had a radio, and this hasn't. And there was a long scratch on the dashboard that Ben did somehow or other, and the window this side wouldn't open all the way down."

"It's quite different then."

"Yes," Ginny said. She looked out of the window and tried to be interested in the passing scenery, but it wasn't at that point very interesting. Fields, hedges, a gas station, a pub, a rash of semidetacheds, a railway station. They passed under a bridge.

"It was my fault," she said. "I should have made him stop. I should have driven for a while and let him rest."

"I see," James said. They drove in silence for another mile.

"Aren't you going to try and reassure me?" Ginny said. "Tell me it wasn't my fault? You are the first person I've told."

"How do I know whose fault it was? I wasn't there. Perhaps it was your fault."

"He wouldn't stop."

"No."

"Oh, James—"

"Go on, have a cry. Why not? There's no one to see."

He didn't look at her. He was watching the road. His profile expressed complete indifference. She didn't know why she had made that sudden plea to him, that impulsive cry of his name for help. He didn't care about her. She was a nuisance he had got landed with for the day.

"I don't want to cry," she said. "I've cried too much. Tell me where we are going."

"To see an old man."

"A relation of yours?"

"No."

"Is Mrs. Sendall a relation of yours? Is she really your aunt?"

"Why," James said, "can't you see the family resemblance?"

"Morgan said he was an only child."

"Morgan knows everything and everybody. I'm surprised he never met your husband. Was the car in good mechanical shape?"

"It had just had an overhaul at the garage."

"That's no indication these days. Which garage?"

"The big one, in North Street."

"There's a coincidence. That's where I hired this car."

"John always went there," Ginny said. "Where does this old man live?"

"On the coast." He turned his head and smiled at her. It was not the consciously charming smile but the other, the one he used to Mrs. Sendall.

"You're doing very well," he said. "If you can't stand it you know, we can go back. I'm not that much of a monster."

"We'll go on," Ginny said. "I don't believe in going back."

They ended up, as James had said and as she might have guessed herself if she'd thought about the direction in which they were traveling, in a town by the sea. It was one of those small towns which began as a fishing village, expanded into a resort in the 1900's, began to die a natural death in the thirties, and was now slowly reviving, transforming itself into a dormitory of London commuters. The man they had come to see lived in the nucleus of the town, in a small stone cottage near the harbor, two rooms downstairs and three upstairs, one of them turned into a bathroom.

"We got a grant to do it," he told them. "A suite of bathroom furniture, they called it. Very nice. My wife wanted pink, and I let her have her way; otherwise she'd have gone on at me about having a garden. I like to be near the boats, you see. I'd be lost up on the hill with the gardening folk. We come from these parts originally. Always been Stones around here. Any street I walk along here I can find a relative. It was my father had the urge to see the world. He moved to Cranesmere and married a local girl. It was a big place then, compared with here. This wasn't much of a place in those days, except in the summers."

He was pleased to have visitors. He'd welcomed them into his house, complete strangers though they were, because James told him he wanted advice on boats, and who better to come to than Mr. F. Stone of Stone's boatyard, now retired. He was a small man, ruddy-faced, friendly and articulate, with the unselfconscious dignity of the craftsman. He was also a born gossip.

"Did you talk to the man running my boatyard now? Bert Taylor? Pshaw!" He dismissed him with a shake of the head. "He's no use. He's got no feeling for it. I hear they're not even doing repairs there now. Can't think why Morgan put him in."

"Taylor doesn't own it then?" James asked.

"No! Morgan bought it from me. Can't think why. He was never interested in boats either that I knew of. But he offered me a fair price, and I wasn't making any money out of it. There was talk once there of building a marina. You know, make it a holiday place, plenty of berths for yachts, dredge the channel, build a sluice so you could come in and out any time you liked and not be stuck with the tides, but that was before the war. Never came to anything. Too lazy or too mean." He laughed. "Cost a bit too much money for Cranesmere, that would. See that council put its hand in its pockets!"

"Is Morgan on the council?" James asked.

"He wasn't then, but he is now. There isn't much he isn't on now. Came up from nothing, you know. His family weren't up to much. His father was a farm laborer. His mother was the one. A schoolteacher when she married, and I reckon it was a case of having to, because I can't see her marrying a laborer unless she had to!" He roared with laughter. "Married beneath her, she thought. Proper ashamed of the old man, they were, her and Jack Morgan —beg his pardon, he likes to be called John now, but it was always Jack in his schooldays."

"So he didn't have any money behind him?" James said.

"Oh, no, there's no money there, except what he's made."

"He's done very well."

"Yes, he's done well for himself. Owns Dent's now. Bought him out, though where he got the money to do that, no one knows. Old man Dent wouldn't have given away his business for chicken feed. He'd have made Morgan pay up."

"Perhaps he borrowed the money."

"Perhaps he did, perhaps he had to. He seems to have plenty to throw around now, any rate. Reckon he plans to buy up the town so they'll have to change its name and call it after him. I'm surprised he's left the boatyard as Stone's. I'd have thought it would be called Morgan's by now!"

"When did he buy Dent's? A long time ago?"

"Oh, no, that's recent history. Only a couple of years ago, if that. His rising in the world's come about quite sudden like. I expect he was working away at it quietly for years. It's just he's out in the open now. He's not as old as he looks, you know. He's quite a young man really. Likes the wine and food too much. And the women!" He laughed again. "Want to watch out for him," he said to Ginny. "Takes after his father in that, anyway."

They went down to the harbor for a drink and to look at the boats.

"What sort are you after?" Stone asked James.

"There's not much here. Fishing vessels mostly, a few sailing dinghies at the yacht club."

"Bert Taylor does fishing trips, doesn't he?" James said. "Could you get far with a boat like his?"

"A fair way. Cross the Channel if you like. Is that what you're after, a bit of smuggling from France? Wouldn't get far with that, you know. Revenue men'd be after you."

"They can't watch all the fishermen," James objected.

"No, but they get to know the ones that go on long voyages, regular ones, and don't report in where they've been, and before you know it, you've got a revenue cutter alongside you, asking awkward questions. And if you try to dodge them, they've got nippy little craft can go up all those creeks and search you out. By God, I believe you are after smuggling! You'd better start looking for a new man, missus, if he starts on that lark. They'll put him away for sure."

Ginny smiled at him. She wondered what James was up to. But when the men eventually went off into long technical discussions about teak versus fiber glass, and diesel engines versus gas, and fifty-fifty motor sailers and converted admiralty craft, she almost began to be persuaded that he had come down here to get advice about boats.

"There're a couple of boatyards not far from here," Stone said. "They'd know what was going around these parts. You'd do better to wait till the winter, though, if you're in no hurry. That's the time to buy boats. I'll come and look them over for you if you like, if you see anything you fancy. Get me there and get me back, and I shan't want anything for doing it. I'll enjoy it."

They shook hands, standing on the cobbled quay.

"By the way," James said, "are Morgan's parents still around in Cranesmere?"

"The old man died about the time Jack Morgan left school," Stone said. "His mother got a teaching post somewhere up London way. She went off, taking Jack

with her. He came back again about two years later, as
far as I remember. I think he went straight into Dent's
and never left them. I don't know where his mother's living or if she's still alive. I did hear a rumor she'd married
again." He cocked a quizzical eye at James. "You're very
interested in friend Morgan, aren't you? What's up? You
after his business?"

James laughed. He did not, however, Ginny noticed,
give Stone an answer.

"Well, good luck to you anyway," Stone said. "And
maybe I'll see you in the winter."

The sea air had given Ginny an appetite. James, too,
apparently, for he tucked her arm under his and guided
her across the ropes and tackle and greasy stones to a bar
on the tourist side of the harbor where they served lobster
and crab and cockles and winkles and anything else in
shells that it might occur to anyone to eat. They had half
a lobster each and draft Guinness, and that, said James,
would either kill or cure her.

"My stomach's not at all delicate," Ginny said. "It's
the strongest part of me."

James leaned his chin on his hand. "It's fascinating.
You're actually licking your lips like a cat."

"Well, it's delicious lobster. Don't you think so?"

"Delicious."

"I like your Mr. F. Stone. I wonder what the F stands
for."

"Frederick," James said.

"You're very well informed. What did you do? Look
up his birth certificate in Somerset House?"

"How sharp you are with me. But what a sensible sug-
gestion. I didn't, as it happened. Information is usually
easier to acquire. As you'll no doubt appreciate after this
morning's chat."

He made her nervous. Her remark about Somerset
House was the direct result of her doubts about his own

background. It was sharp, and a silly thing to say, but he made her react in foolish ways. He continued to gaze at her across the table. He had said she licked her lips like a cat, but it was he who was feline. He had eyes like a cat. The wrong color but the right shape, the right veiled, mysterious, watchful expression. Alice's eyes were a golden amber, James' blue, but she had met the same gaze in both.

"Are you trying to hypnotize me?" she asked.

"I like looking at you," he said. "The pale skin, the fragility, the delicate bones, the enormous appetite. You fascinate me."

"I don't know what to make of you."

"I don't know what to make of you. Why did you come and live with my aunt?"

"She asked me to."

"You had a perfectly good house. Ben was quite happy at his school. So why put it up for sale and move?"

"James, it's none of your business."

"Isn't it?" he said. "Did Morgan advise you to move?"

"Morgan? For heaven's sake! I'd never even met Morgan till I came to live with Mrs. Sendall. And I can't stand the man."

"He likes you, though, doesn't he? He has an eye for women, Stone said. He must have seen you in the town many times. Your husband must have met him. He did know him, didn't he? He went to the bookshop Morgan owned. He had his car serviced at the garage Morgan owned."

Ginny stared at him. "I didn't know Morgan owned that garage. What are you getting at? James, what are you doing to me?" Her eyes had filled with tears.

He sighed. He put his hand on hers. "Bear with me, Ginny."

"I know," she said. "You're not the monster you appear. But to me you are. It no longer seems such a good idea Mrs. Sendall had—to send me out for a healthy ride. The cure hurts more than the complaint."

"I'm sorry," he said. "I'm very insensitive to other people's feelings, as you've noticed."

"Yes," she said.

"But there are reasons. There are always reasons, aren't there?" He squeezed her hand. "Come on, I'll take you home."

They didn't talk on the drive back. James left her in peace, nor did he drive fast but took the winding road around the coast, approaching Cranesmere at last by a lonely country road which traversed a featureless landscape of fields and marshes, crossed by dikes. They passed through a hamlet: two houses, a pub with a bus waiting outside. Ginny sat up.

"What is it?" James said.

"Nothing. I suddenly recognized where we were. Ben and I came for a picnic here. The day you arrived."

The car slowed to a halt. James reversed, turned, and drove back to the pub.

"Now what are you doing?" Ginny demanded.

"I want you to show me where you went."

"Oh, really, James!"

"I'm serious."

"But what for? It's miles. I don't want to go trekking over the countryside, just to amuse you."

"It's not for amusement."

She shook her head. "No. I'm sorry, but no."

"Are you frightened to walk across those empty fields with me, is that it?"

"No, that's not it, but now I come to think of it, wouldn't I be wise to be wary? I know nothing whatever about you."

"I know nothing about you," he said.

"Well, that's hardly the point, is it?"

"Are you coming, or aren't you?"

"No!"

"Right." He took her by the shoulders and kissed her. She was too surprised to resist.

"And what," she said, regaining her breath, "was that for?"

"You're beautiful, and your husband's dead, and you need kissing."

Then Ginny became really angry. "I don't need your kisses. I don't need your particular brand of male arrogance. My husband may be dead, but to me he's still very much alive, and I'll be glad if you'll leave me alone and stay out of my affairs."

"So you're going to be a professional widow, is that it? Is that why you left your house and your home and became a lodger in another woman's house?"

"Shut up, James."

"You've got to stop mourning some day. You can't escape from your own life so easily. You're going to see cars that look like this, and men are going to want to kiss you, and Ben is going to need his own home——"

She clenched her fist and struck at his arm. "I'm not mourning! I'm not, I'm not! If I could only remember, I could forget, I could sleep. I have forgotten. I had forgotten. I had let him go. . . ." Her voice died away. She let her hand lie where it was, against his arm. He took it in his own hands and uncurled the fingers, one by one.

"You weren't responsible for his death," he said. "Everyone thinks that after an accident. You could have changed places and driven the car, and it could have been you who fell asleep and died. You can't control these things. Stop blaming yourself."

She didn't reply. He hadn't helped her, if that was what he had intended. He had made things worse.

After a while he spoke again. "I didn't mean to say many of those things. I don't know why I did. I didn't know I was going to kiss you. It was an impulse. I didn't mean to hurt you. I'm sorry."

"Well"—Ginny endeavored to smile—"it doesn't matter. To quote you: Stop blaming yourself. Let's go on, shall we?"

"Of course." He turned the car, and they drove on to Cranesmere. And Ginny never remembered to ask him exactly why he had wanted to see where Ben and she had had their picnic.

In the quiet of the evening, Mrs. Sendall was walking in her garden. How full it was of delicious scents. The white-starred jasmine clinging to the trellis, the dark dropping roses, the stocks, the acrid-smelling hollyhocks which always seemed to her to hold the taste of dust no matter how fleshily fragile the wrinkled petals of their trumpets—she breathed their mingled fragrances with pleasure and enjoyed as much the progression from their sweetness to the earthy warmth of rotting weeds by the garden wall. As she approached, Alice rose courteously from her evening doze to greet her, swaying along the path of crumbling bricks with surefooted delicacy. Mrs. Sendall tickled her gently in the ruff of fur beneath the chin, and the cat turned her head, pressing her cheek hard against the caressing hand in a quiet and familiar ecstasy.

Into the silence came the murmur of voices. Mrs. Sendall gave Alice a final affectionate pat and went, impelled by nothing more than vulgar curiosity, to the gate in the wall. She opened it and stepped through. On the other side of the wall, an old man was on his knees in the allotments, planting out seedling lettuces. Beside him in a basket were the several fat round ones he had already plucked. Sitting on a box talking to him was James.

"Hello, Mr. Laycock!" Mrs. Sendall called. The old man looked around and raised a hand in acknowledgment.

She walked over the soft earth toward them. The long day was fading to a purple dusk, Mediterranean in its luminosity. The house behind her glowed, as if giving out in this last hour all the sunlight absorbed during the day.

"Like some lettuces for your salad?" Mr. Laycock asked.

"How kind! What beauties! I'd love some." She had lettuces running to seed in her own garden, but she could not bear to refuse him. Apart from anything else, to do so would mean to watch them rotting from the window along with so many other neglected vegetables.

"Mr. Laycock was telling me he's giving up the allotment," James said.

"Indeed? I'm sorry to hear that."

"I was telling your nephew," the old man explained. "The council have offered me another plot, nearer home. It's a long trudge up here when you're getting on."

"I shall miss you," Mrs. Sendall said. "You know you're one of the few people who still come here. It won't be the same without you."

"Last of the old faithfuls." He grunted. "I won't say it isn't peaceful here. But nobody cares anymore, do they? Look at it! Look at all the weeds spreading everywhere."

"And the ants," Mrs. Sendall said feelingly.

"Lonely place," he said. "You should visit your auntie more often." He spoke quite strongly to James. "Too quiet and lonely up here. And when they shut it down—"

"Are they going to shut it down?" Mrs. Sendall inquired.

"Stands to reason, doesn't it? I'm one of the last. They've found me a plot elsewhere. Who's going to keep these great allotments going? And when they shut it down—" he repeated.

"All the peace will vanish," James remarked.

"What did you mean by that?" Mrs. Sendall asked James as they walked back to the house.

"If they are giving up the allotments, the council intends to do something else with them," James replied. "Stands to reason, as Mr. Laycock said. I think they'll sell the land for building."

Mrs. Sendall stopped short. "Do you really think so?"

"Think what this land would be worth for building."

"Would it really be worth so much?" Mrs. Sendall wondered. "Half Mr. Morgan's nasty flats are still unlet, you know. I don't think people want to live so far out of the town."

"On an island the size of ours," James said, "all land is building land in the end."

"What a pessimist you are."

"You won't like it, will you? Rows of houses at the bottom of your garden?"

"I've got a nice big garden. I'm not such a dog in the manger as all that, I hope. I shan't mind them—" She broke off. "I shan't mind them as long as it's not Morgan building them, and as it's very likely to be him, I might as well agree that I'd hate that. I've taken such a dislike to that man."

James slashed absentmindedly at a poppy head. "I don't think it will be houses, I think it's planned for something else." He stopped. "The more I think about it, the clearer the pattern becomes."

"Well, it's not clear to me," Mrs. Sendall said. "And stop damaging my flowers."

"Where's Ginny?" James asked.

"Upstairs with Ben, I think. Did you want to see her?"

"No. It didn't go terribly well today."

"So I gathered," she said dryly.

"Why," James said. "What did she say?"

"She didn't say anything. That's how I know it didn't go well. James, I'm afraid I made a mistake asking you to take her with you. She's got that lost look in her eyes again."

"You're wrong. It was a very excellent idea." He spoke encouragingly. "You've taken her under your wing. It's as much as you can do. She's got to do the rest. Here, give me those lettuces." He took them from her and carried them into the kitchen.

"I shan't be in tonight," he said. "I'm going to London."

She regarded him inquiringly. "I see."

"I want to be there first thing, outside several doors."

"Very well, dear boy, be enigmatic. It suits you anyway."

He laughed. "Dear Aunt Cissie." He paused. "Take care of Ginny, won't you? No more homicidal cats turning on gas taps."

"Anyone would think," Mrs. Sendall said, "you were in love with the girl."

It was disconcerting for Ginny to find James gone the next morning. She was as uneasy at his absence as she had been in his presence. Mrs. Sendall was no help. She was as vague as ever about his whereabouts.

"But is he coming back?" Ginny asked.

"As far as I know. You don't look well, dear. You're not thinking of going to work, are you?"

"If I don't go soon, I won't have a job to go to."

"Surely not."

"I know the signs. I'm not indispensable. So I think I will go today. That is, if you're not too tired of coping with Ben."

"Of course I'll cope. But I still think it's too soon to go back."

"I'm really quite all right," Ginny said. "It's just that I'm not sleeping very well."

"I am sorry. Should you take a sleeping pill occasionally, do you think?"

Ginny shook her head.

"To tide you over."

"No." Ginny tried to explain. "When I do sleep, I get a worrying kind of dream. I'd rather not dream it. I don't mind about losing sleep."

"A dream about the accident?"

"Yes." She dismissed it, pouring tea, buttering toast, picking up one of the morning papers, and folding it back ready to read. She looked up to find Mrs. Sendall watching her. "I have a blank, you see, in my memory about the accident. I find it worrying. I wish I could remember, that's all. It must be causing the dream, the effort to remember. When I do, the dream will stop and I'll sleep. That's all there is to it."

"Ginny—"

"Dear Mrs. Sendall, don't be too sympathetic, just this minute. I find it very undermining." She paused. "Do you think it's going to work, our being here? Do you think I acted too impulsively uprooting Ben? There's something bothering him. He's been sleeping so restlessly these past few nights. Muttering in his sleep. He's usually up by now, tearing around the place. It must mean he's not sleeping properly during the night."

Mrs. Sendall was pretty sure she knew what was upsetting Ben. His father dead and his mother nearly killed by gas; accident or no accident, the effect on Ben was the same. She could hardly alarm Ginny by going into all that. Ginny herself gave her enough concern. She looked so frail and vulnerable this morning. She didn't know who to blame the more, herself or James. James, she decided firmly. He was the one who rented the car.

"I don't think it's anything much with Ben," she said in a way both as comforting and offhand as she could manage. "If I get a chance today, I'll see if I can find out. The business with the tramp upset him, didn't it? He may have had a nightmare or something."

"The tramp. Of course." Ginny felt relieved. That was a matter that could be talked about, soothed away, helped. To know the cause behind a child's fears was half the battle.

Strangely enough, the tramp cropped up again that morning at the shop. Ginny got back from lunch to find Eileen holding court with her fiancé. This was a young man Ginny had not met before, and she could see at once he was no match for the formidable Eileen. He gazed at her with wonder and admiration; he was overwhelmed by her, and one day, Ginny foresaw, when it all became too much for him, he would run off with a little blond typist and Eileen would never understand why.

His name was Tom. He was twenty-three years old and worked on the local newspaper.

When he was introduced to her, there was such a noticeable leap of interest in his eyes, his attention so quickly diverted from Eileen to herself, that for the first time Ginny began to wonder about other people's attitudes toward her.

Her reception when she arrived for work at the shop, for instance. Mrs. Levison-Wrightly putting her arm around her, inquiring almost tenderly how she was; Mrs. Craig providing her with more cups of coffee than she could possibly manage to drink; Eileen regarding her with a mixture of amazement and awe. There had been an aura of excitement in the shop, and she realized now that she had been the cause and the center of it. It suddenly came to her that they all thought she had tried to commit suicide. At once everyone else's reaction became clear. She was astonished at what a fool she had been not to see it before. She was both angry and relieved. Angry because it would be impossible to broach the subject, to go up to someone and say, "But didn't you know, couldn't you see that I never could do that? Do you think I care so little for Ben?" Relieved because the atmosphere had been puzzling her and now it was explained.

She could almost feel Eileen's young man teetering on the edge of the appalling *faux pas* of asking her why she had done it and how it felt to come back from the dead.

"How is the paper?" she said, to help him. "I'm afraid I don't often see it."

"Quite exciting," he said. He was an attractive boy, smiling and eager. He had a round face and soft fair hair.

"Tell her about the tramp," Eileen commanded.

He glanced at her and then around at the three or four

customers at their end of the shop, half listening, half sorting through clothes racks. He was a trifle disturbed. "It's not released yet."

"Oh, come on! Ginny won't tell."

"What about the tramp?" Ginny asked.

Eileen brushed Tom's continued hesitation aside impatiently. "Someone did him in. Isn't it weird? They bashed the poor old drunk over the head with the proverbial blunt instrument and pushed him into the barge out of the way."

"You mean he was murdered?"

"Honestly, Eileen," her fiancé protested. "It was confidential."

She took his hand. "Darling, don't fuss. Isn't he beautiful, Ginny? Aren't I a lucky girl?" She kissed his cheek. He looked fond but embarrassed.

"I won't repeat it," Ginny assured him. "Did the police tell you?"

"They told my editor. He sent me to try and find out more about the man."

"And have you?"

"Not yet. They think it was a quarrel about drink. He was probably hit with a bottle. It's not really all that interesting, you know. A scuffle that went too far. Not like a deliberate murder."

"Don't be so gloomy," Eileen said. "It may be sordid, but it's news. It'll be your story the paper prints when it is released, and then all the nationals will be after it, and your name will be known, and before you know it, Fleet Street, here we come!"

"Do you want to go to Fleet Street?" Ginny asked him.

"Who doesn't?" But it was not wholly convincing. He was clearly happy as he was, and if he stayed where he was, in his small and friendly pond, he'd no doubt end up as quite a big fish. It was a pity, Ginny thought, that he was going to be pushed and maneuvered away.

"Are there many tramps around here?" she asked.

"No. You don't want to worry about it, Mrs. Benson. Whoever was involved will have moved on in a hurry. I shouldn't think there are any around here at the moment. News of trouble spreads fast. They'll all be gone." He was concerned to reassure her. He had more imagination than Eileen, considering they all thought Ginny to be unstable. She decided she liked him a lot and told Eileen so when he had gone.

"Do you? I am glad. I adore him. His only fault is that he's a bit slow and dreamy. But with me behind him—oh, I forgot! You'll murder me. Your boyfriend rang from London. Robert Travis."

"When? What did he want?"

"He wouldn't tell me, and don't think I didn't ask. He rang just after you'd left for lunch, and he's ringing back any minute now."

"That sounds urgent."

"Yes," Eileen agreed. "He did sound urgent. I'm dying of curiosity."

The afternoon crawled by. It was nearly five o'clock before Robert rang again. Ginny took the call in the storeroom, closing the door behind the ubiquitous Eileen. For no good reason she could think of she was terribly nervous.

"Robert?"

"Is that you, Ginny? Thank goodness. Look, I'm on my way back. Can you meet me? About seven, in the pub near the shop. I've got to talk to you."

"What's happened?" Ginny asked.

"Where's Aldous? Is he at the house?"

"I think he's in London. Anyway, he left last night, and no one knows when he'll be back."

"That's a relief. Let's hope he never comes back."

"Robert, what is it? What have you found out about him?"

"Whatever I tell you, Ginny, don't tell Mrs. Sendall. Not until I've seen you."

"All right, I won't say anything. But what is it? You're making me very worried. Was Morgan right? Hasn't Mrs. Sendall got a nephew?"

"She's got a nephew all right," Robert said. "Her brother's son. He went to live in Vancouver with his parents when he was ten years old. He's still there. I've just been talking to him. He hasn't seen his aunt or visited her for twenty years. He's never left Canada since he was ten years old."

Ginny stood, clutching the phone. She heard herself say, "Then who is—"

"Who, indeed?" said Robert. "And what, exactly, is he up to?"

Mrs. Sendall put down the phone and went back into the living room. Ben was sitting exactly where she had left him, watching television, but she had the strong impression he had been listening at the door.

"That was your mother," she said equably. "She doesn't think she'll be here for supper. So we won't wait."

Ben nodded. He followed her obediently to the kitchen and sat in his usual seat at the table. He ate his supper in silence.

"What's the matter, Ben?" she said at last.

He looked up, his eyes guarded. "Nothing."

"Well, something's the matter," she commented, briskly disposing of dirty dishes in a flurry of soapy water. "Is it the tramp?"

There was a stricken silence behind her. She turned. The boy was staring at her, an expression of such horror on his face that even she was quite shocked.

"Why, Ben! Why, my dear, what is it?"

He continued to gaze at her with that distorted, terrified look and then suddenly leaped from his chair and ran across the kitchen to her, flinging his arms around her waist, burying his head in the folds of her apron. He was sobbing and shouting at the same time. "I killed him, but he's not dead. He keeps coming back for me; he keeps coming back looking for me."

She held him and rocked him and settled him on her knee, and at length she got the story out of him. The visits to the church, the tramp in the pulpit and his fall down the stairs, the finding of his body in the barge, the figure he had seen coming up the garden at night, the footsteps in the house, his mother nearly dead—

"I see," Mrs. Sendall said. "You thought he had come for you and found your mother and made do with her."

"Not really," he said. He had stopped crying. He was serious, in deadly earnest. "I knew he wouldn't really harm her, only me. But it seemed funny. And then he was here again, last night."

It was Mrs. Sendall's turn to stare. "Are you sure?"

"I heard him," Ben said. "He was walking about the house, looking for me."

"That's not your tramp," Mrs. Sendall said staunchly. She had had a bright idea. "That was our own common or garden ghost. You see, I didn't tell you about him in case your mother got frightened. But he's an old gentleman who used to live here and liked it so much he doesn't want to leave. He's quite harmless. He would never hurt anyone. Your tramp can't come back. He's safely buried. He might have come that once, but not anymore. You can be quite sure of that. And you didn't kill him, Ben. He didn't die until the night before you found him. So, you see, he has no reason to come after you. You are quite safe from him."

She wondered if it was going to work, such a tissue of lies and so full of holes. He was silent and tense, and then he said, "Have you really got a ghost?"

She took a breath and hoped the Lord would forgive yet another lie. "Yes, Ben, a dear sweet gentleman, just as I said. So don't let any noises in the house worry you ever again."

It appeared to work. He quieted down, and though he

remained thoughtful, he teased Alice when she slipped in through her cat door in quite the old infuriating manner. But he had left Mrs. Sendall immensely alarmed. She had no doubt he had heard someone the evening before. Hadn't she heard something herself that other evening? Who was it who was coming into the house? What were they looking for? And with James and Ginny away, how could she protect Ben if the intruder should come again tonight?

When they had cleared away the supper things, she took Ben upstairs to her room. She wanted to distract him. "I've got something you might like to see."

From the top of a wardrobe, she pulled down a leather case and opened it. To Ben's delight, it was full of a collection of extraordinary things: beautiful glass marbles; brown and curling photographs of soldiers in strange uniforms, posed near palm trees; a curved knife in a curved sheath, richly decorated; an ivory fan; silken scarves, all colors; and a fine cashmere shawl which Mrs. Sendall demonstrated could be drawn through a wedding ring.

"Wait!" Ben cried, dashing along the corridor. "See what I've got!" One display of treasure deserved another. He drew the precious attaché case from under his bed and carried it to Mrs. Sendall's room. He opened it proudly and drew the objects out one by one: the bird's skull, the feathers, the pottery, the pebbles—

Mrs. Sendall sat frozen in her chair, staring at the pebbles. She put out a tentative hand and picked one up, then another. She counted them in an awestruck whisper. Eight of them. Eight! And the size of them. No wonder, she thought. No wonder.

"Ben," she said in a voice that trembled, "where did you find these?"

"In the church," he said.

"Were they loose, like this?"

"Oh, no, they were in a paper bag. But I lost that."

"And this is all there were?"

"Yes, they were all together." She sounded a bit odd. "Is anything wrong, Mrs. Sendall?"

"No, dear, no, no, nothing at all."

Her gaze alighted on another object among his treasures. One that had seemed so unimportant but that now frightened her even more than the pebbles. "Where did you find the cigarette, Ben? The one with the pretty gold band."

"In the church, too. I found another one there once, but I lost it."

Yes, Mrs. Sendall thought, I swept it up in my dustpan. She sat still, thinking desperately what to do. The plan she finally concocted and instructed Ben in, pretending to him that it was a game, was simple and as desperate as her fears, and it required a lot of courage from them both. But it was done at last, and she came back to her room again to wait.

He came early, sooner than she expected, as if he knew he would find them alone, as if he had grown careless and impatient in his search. She heard the steps, faintly moving the floorboards, and they stopped, as she had been afraid they would, by Ben's door. She left her room. He had taken the bulb from the corridor light. When she pressed the switch, nothing happened. And now he had heard her. He came toward her along the passage. She held her ground. She spoke aloud to the shadows.

"I know who you are," she said. "And I know what you want."

❧ 6 ❧

ROBERT ARRIVED LATE. It was half past seven before he came into the bar of the pub.

"I'm sorry." He took Ginny's hand. "I was held up. How are you?"

"Worried," she said. "Are you sure it's true?"

He sank down on to the bench beside her and waved for a drink. "Quite sure. As I told you, I spoke to the genuine nephew. You haven't told Mrs. Sendall?"

"No, I've said nothing. I haven't been home yet. What are we supposed to do? Call the police?"

"He hasn't done anything actually criminal yet as far as we know. I think we have to leave any action of that sort to Mrs. Sendall. What do you want to drink?"

Ginny shook her head. She already had a full glass. She watched Robert while he took his drink and paid for it. He lifted the glass in salute to her before drinking. He was drinking whiskey. It was unusual. He usually drank beer.

"You look as if you needed that," Ginny remarked.

"I did. I'm as worried as hell about all this, Ginny. What's the point of it? A con job, we know, but what's he after? Is she very rich?"

"I don't think so. I'm sure she isn't. She's living on a pension from her husband, I believe, though she might have some money of her own. She looks after the house and garden herself. But, Robert, you know the situation. You've been to the house."

"Yes." He was frowning at the table.

"How did you find out?" She was thinking of James: the charm, the watchfulness, the questions.

"It wasn't difficult. What took the time was finding the telephone number in Canada."

"I think that was very clever. I would never have thought of that."

"Did he say anything to you? Anything that might give us a clue?"

"He asked me questions. Now I think of it, he was suspicious of me, almost hostile." Could you call that kiss hostile, she wondered.

"As if he thought you might spoil his plans, as if you were another interloper?"

"Yes, it could be."

"Perhaps she has jewelry. Old ladies often have things tucked away, diamond brooches, rings, old tiaras."

Ginny smiled; it was such a delightful picture, Mrs. Sendall dressed to the nines and wearing a tiara. And it was quite possible too.

"I don't know. We'll ask when we get back. Robert, you would think she would know he wasn't her nephew."

"Not if she hadn't seen him for twenty years."

"James would be too young, wouldn't he?"

He shrugged.

"Perhaps we should go back now to warn her," Ginny said. "After all, he might come back. He might be back already."

"No." He finished his drink. "We'll eat first."

"But do you think—"

"Yes, I really think." He kissed her cheek. "Come on."

There were two hotels in the town, one cramped and Tudor, with a heavily faked steak bar tacked on to one corner, the other Georgian, drafty and prim. They chose the second, since the only alternatives to the small burned offerings the steak bar provided were the bland, flavorless dishes of an indifferent Chinese restaurant or fish-and-chips. They sat in a corner of the echoing dining room and ate their way through three tepid courses.

"Oh, for a restaurant that serves you real roast beef," Ginny sighed, "all brown and rich on the outside and pink inside, served with its own juices, or real roast lamb, Welsh lamb, that melts in the mouth." She turned over her piece of dried-up chicken. "No wonder we all eat at home."

"The one thing to avoid in the country, I've learned," Robert said, "is candles. If you walk into a restaurant and see a cluster of imported waiters in evening dress, serving meals by candlelight with a great many silver dishes, walk straight out again. The ambience may be divine, but the food will be uneatable. Would you like something else?"

"No. I'm not hungry. I think I'd like some more wine. It's very good."

Robert agreed. "The English have always known how to drink."

He was in his man-of-the-world mood, Ginny noticed; earlier he had been as tense and worried as she was. Only she was more than worried. She was shocked; it was a word with many meanings, and each one was applicable to her present state. She had a sick feeling in her stomach, and it wasn't caused by the poor food or too much wine.

"I think we ought to go back," she said.

Robert looked at his watch. "When we've finished the wine."

"I think it's Morgan," Ginny said.

There was a pause before Robert said quietly, dropping

all affectation, "What do you mean, you think it's Morgan?"

"Well, something to do with him, anyway. Quite a lot of James' questions, I've remembered, had to do with Morgan. He was interested in everything about him, the boatyard he's bought, the bookshop, everything. I think he might be in the same line. You know, a property speculator or something. Mr. Morgan is, after all, owner of the largest estate agency here, isn't he?"

"I see," Robert said. He thought about it in silence. "Yes, I suppose that is one explanation. Perhaps the confidence trick is going to be on Morgan. We ought to warn him James Aldous isn't what he seems."

"I hadn't thought of that aspect of it," Ginny said. "I meant he might be spying out the land incognito, that's all."

"Whatever he does will be tricky," Robert said. "We can bet on that."

They left the hotel about ten and drove back to the house. If Mrs. Sendall was still up, they would tell her about her pseudo nephew then and there; if she had gone to bed, Ginny said there was no point in waking her up to tell her.

"How did it go in London apart from this?" Ginny asked. "Did you get the rest of your business done?"

"It went quite well."

"I never asked you," Ginny said, "if you are on holiday. Or don't you need to work?"

"I need to work all right," Robert said, apparently unoffended by what Ginny considered her nosiness. "But not right this minute. I came by some money from a relative a few months ago. That's why I was thinking of starting a bookshop. Whether or not the capital would be enough I haven't quite worked out yet. If I do take the shop, perhaps you'd come and work for me."

"Perhaps."

"I'd see you had your lunch hour at the same time every day."

"Well, that's quite an inducement, I must say."

"And had all school holidays off."

"And pay me a wage as well? I can't believe it."

"I wouldn't pay you for long. I'd soon think of some arrangement that didn't depend on money. Something simple like bed and board, for instance."

She was silent.

"I'm sorry," he said.

Ginny laughed. "Oh, Robert!"

The house was in darkness when they drew up outside it, except for an odd flickering light visible through the uncurtained windows of the living room. It took Ginny a moment or two to realize it was the television.

"Mrs. Sendall doesn't usually watch it in complete darkness," she said. "She generally keeps a light on."

"Perhaps she went to bed and forgot to turn it off."

"More than likely." She got out her key. "Would you like to come in for a drink. Some of the illicit James' gin?"

"Most certainly I would."

Ginny unlocked the front door and they went inside. They crossed the hall to the living room and Ginny switched on the light. They were met with a scene of devastation.

The room had been ransacked. Chairs and tables were overturned, the carpet pulled back, upholstery slashed, books swept off shelves and tumbled on the floor, the drawers of a bureau emptied, even Mrs. Sendall's knitting had been attacked, the basket knocked over and needles and wools scattered.

Robert stared. "Good God!"

"Ben!" Ginny fled upstairs and flung open his door. It was the same story, the drawers of the chest wrenched out, their contents tossed everywhere, Ben's clothes pulled from the wardrobe, his collection of treasures spilled over the rug. But Ben at least was unruffled. In the middle of the chaos, he lay fast asleep in his bed. Even the flood of light failed to wake him. She switched the light off and pulled the door to, bumping into Robert, who had come up behind her from the stairs. It was dark in the corridor.

"He's all right," she whispered. "He's asleep."

"Do you think Mrs. Sendall could have slept through it too?"

"There must have been a lot of noise. Surely not."

"In that case, where is she?"

"Let's see."

He tried the switch. "The light's gone."

Ginny had moved ahead along the corridor toward Mrs. Sendall's room. A moment later Robert heard a gasp and a stifled cry.

He ran forward blindly and found Ginny clinging to him. "There's something there, on the floor. I stumbled over it."

They had found Mrs. Sendall.

Concussion, the doctor told them. Mrs. Sendall had been struck a savage blow on the head with a weapon such as a bar or a heavy torch and sustained further bruising when she fell to the floor. She was unconscious, and concussion being such a tricky business, he could not say when she would recover consciousness. He had also looked at the boy, and in his opinion the child had been given a sleeping pill. Let him sleep it off. He was untouched otherwise.

The house seemed full of people, though there were in fact only two policemen, the ambulance men, and the doctor. Ginny and Robert had dialed 999 and asked for both services. Then they had called Mrs. Sendall's doctor. When the doctor had finished his preliminary examination, Ginny watched her friend wrapped in blankets and carried out of the house on a stretcher. She looked such a tiny, pathetic figure; the experience left Ginny angry and tearful. She was torn between a wish to go with her to the hospital and look after her, though she knew she could do no more than wait around in a hospital corridor, and her desire to be with Ben.

The sleeping pill business alarmed her. Had this been Mrs. Sendall's habit to ensure a quiet evening when Ginny was out? It seemed totally against character. Then why do it, this one time? Had she known something was going to happen? Something to do with James?

"Next of kin?" the young detective sergeant inquired. He was a plump country lad from the local CID.

Ginny and Robert exchanged glances.

"She has a nephew," Ginny said at last. "James Aldous. At least, he said he was her nephew. We have reason to believe—" She cleared her throat, wondering in a moment of panic if the sergeant would think she was making fun of police phraseology. But how else could you say it? "We think he's an impostor. Mr. Travis has spoken to Mrs. Sendall's nephew, and he is in Canada where he's been for the past twenty years."

And now you've done it, she thought. Now the betrayal is on both sides. But what was he after? What could be worth such brutality?

Robert was talking. He was telling the policeman about his investigations into James' identity. Ginny yearned to get back upstairs to Ben in case he did wake and was frightened.

"Have you any idea what was taken?" the sergeant asked her.

She shook her head. "At the first look around, nothing I know about is missing. Things I've seen about the house, I mean. Ornaments, silver and so on. That's odd, isn't it? And nothing seems to be gone from my own room. My engagement ring, which I wasn't wearing tonight and is the only valuable thing I possess, that's still there. I don't know what was hidden, of course. If Mrs. Sendall had money or jewels put away."

"They sometimes get that idea," the sergeant nodded. "Old ladies living alone must be sitting on a fortune. It's common enough."

"Could it be tramps?"

"Possibly. A certain kind. Most tramps are harmless."

Ginny felt a slight stir of relief. "It might not be James Aldous then?"

"Con men are rarely violent," the sergeant said. "We shall be investigating, of course. You don't know where he is?"

"Mrs. Sendall would know."

"Mrs. Sendall might be very informative if she were only conscious and able to speak." He folded his notebook. "I think that's all at the moment. You'll be hearing from us. And let us know if you find anything missing."

"How did he get in?" she asked.

"Window at the back. Easy enough. No proper locks, as far as I can see." He seemed displeased at this laxity.

They were left with the chaos. Robert went around picking up furniture, putting books back on shelves. Ginny made coffee. Even here in the kitchen, jars of flour and sugar and rice had been opened and stirred about. It was this fact that convinced her the burglar or burglars had been after jewelry. An inexperienced person would imagine a tin of flour a safe place to hide jewels. Obviously, thieves knew that too.

Poor Mrs. Sendall, had she some diamonds or emeralds, relics of her happy marriage? Had she, with the confidence you would have in a relative, talked to James about them? And had James slipped back and robbed her and nearly killed her and fled away again?

Robert came into the kitchen and put an arm about her shoulders. "Don't look so stricken. She'll be all right."

"Will they catch him?"

"They'll catch him."

She wouldn't let him stay for long. It was very late, and she was desperately tired. She would clean up the rest of the mess in the morning.

When he had gone, she went upstairs and into Ben's room. He had not moved an inch from his former position. He did not stir while she gathered up his things and began to put them into some order. When the room was tidy again, she fetched a pillow and a blanket from her own room and dozed in a chair beside the bed. She woke at six, stiff and bemused. Ben slept on, pink and cherubic, looking as he had done when he was four and no clouds had troubled their world.

Ginny rang the hospital and was told with slight reproof that it was too early for news. There had been no change in Mrs. Sendall's condition during the night. The doctor would be calling to see her later.

She went upstairs and had a bath to wake herself up, the window flung open to the morning birdcalls. She put on jeans and a shirt, twisted her hair into a bun, drank three cups of tea standing at the kitchen table, and then got down to cleaning up the house. She scrubbed floors and dusted and polished and swept, driven by an instinctive desire to obliterate all traces of the intruder. The ravaging of the house had had an obscene quality. She wanted to make it clean, pure, untarnished as a gift for Mrs. Sendall.

As soon as the shop was open, she telephoned Mrs. Levison-Wrightly. The proprietress was horrified by the news, which it soon transpired, she had already heard from the efficient town grapevine. Shortly afterward Eileen arrived with fiancé Tom in tow, and was clearly mortified to find nothing left for her to do.

"Mrs. L. W. sent us up to see if we could help. They didn't make much mess, did they?"

Ben was up by now and sitting at the kitchen table, all ears. He had no idea, Ginny had discovered, thanks to her early-morning activities, that anything at all had happened in the house the previous night. She had asked him, in a carefully casual manner, what he had done last night.

"Watched the telly," he said. "Played games."

"What sort of games?"

"Hide-and-seek mostly. Mum, did you know we had a ghost?"

"Ghost! What sort of a ghost?"

"An old gentleman. He walks about the house at night. He likes living here so much he won't go away, Mrs. Sendall says. So you're not to be frightened if you hear him. Where is Mrs. Sendall, Mum?"

"She's had to go and see a friend who's not very well," Ginny said. "She'll be away for a little while."

Ben digested this information.

"She didn't say good-bye."

"She had to go in a bit of a rush. She asked me to say good-bye for her."

"Are you going to work, Mum?"

"No, Ben. Not for a few days."

"Can we go for a picnic?"

"We'll see."

That remark sometimes meant yes, but Ben was sufficiently experienced with women by now to know that this time it meant no. He was philosophical about it. He considered other means of entertainment.

"Where's Alice?"

"I haven't seen her this morning. In the garden, I expect. Have you had enough breakfast? Do you want to go in the garden?"

It was at this point that Eileen and Tom arrived. Ben, half out of his chair, climbed back on it and waited on events.

"What a terrible thing!" Eileen cried. "How is she? Have you heard? And Ben slept through it. What a blessing!" She gazed at Ben with a dramatic stare registering horror and amazement. Ben sat up, becoming rapidly more interested. He looked inquiringly at his mother.

"Yes," Ginny said, avoiding him. "Ben didn't hear the phone call. Mrs. Sendall had to rush off to her friend first thing. I expect we'll see how she's getting on soon enough."

Eileen turned to her with genuine astonishment written on her face. Tom nudged her. Ben waited.

"Let's go into the other room," Ginny said. "Ben, why don't you go into the garden and look for Alice?"

A great "ooh" of understanding emerging from Eileen nearly wrecked even this simple subterfuge, but Ben became bored as soon as they moved into the living room and, after listening to a few minutes of trivial chatter about the shop, drifted through the french windows into the garden.

Eileen immediately became effusively apologetic. "Oh, my God, I'm sorry, Ginny! What an idiot I am. I've no imagination. Isn't that true, Tom? So Ben didn't hear anything. Wasn't that strange, but what a good thing! They might have killed him, mightn't they? Will the old lady recover?"

"They say it's concussion," Ginny said. She felt enfeebled by the effort of lying to Ben, by Eileen's curiosity.

"What were they after? What have they taken? Money?"

"That's what's odd. I can't find anything missing."

"You didn't mind me bringing Tom, did you? You don't mind if he takes notes and things? I said she wouldn't mind, Tom. It's more like family when you know the person, isn't it?"

"She means she thought you wouldn't mind talking about the burglary if she came too," Tom explained. "But I quite understand if you don't want to talk about it. I've already spoken to the police, but it's always good to have a direct quote if you can."

"I don't mind if the police don't." Ginny told him what she knew, which amounted to very little. "Don't mention Ben, will you?" she asked him. "I want to keep him out of it if possible."

"Tom knew your husband," Eileen said. "Didn't you, Tom?"

Ginny had forgotten what unexpected remarks like that could do to her. She said brightly, "Did you, Tom? I didn't know."

"I remembered when I heard your surname. Eileen had only referred to you as Ginny before," Tom said. "It was only once. At the police station as a matter of fact. He came in about something while I was there. You could hardly say I knew him. I probably wouldn't have remembered the incident at all except for doing the report on"—he hesitated, obviously regretting that Eileen had brought the matter up—"on the accident. You get in the habit of remembering names and faces. Ben's very like him, isn't he?"

"Yes," Ginny agreed. "I wonder what that was about, his going to the station, I mean."

"Motoring fine, I expect," Eileen said. "It usually is. Well!" She stood up. "If you're sure there's nothing I can do to help. Back to the salt mines. You're not coming in, of course. You stay away as long as you can. Make sure the old girl pays you, though. She's mean enough to sack you for a couple of weeks and take you back on afterward, all smiles. Come on, Tom."

The detective sergeant arrived about fifteen minutes later. He appeared slightly taken aback by the spotless condition of the house.

"You've been very thorough."

Ginny was struck by an awful thought. "I wasn't supposed to leave it as it was, was I? I haven't wiped away all the clues?"

"No, we had finished. We did tell you to clear up if you wished. If you remember."

"That's a relief."

"I was surprised how quickly you'd tidied up. It looks very nice."

"Thank you."

"Discovered anything missing yet?"

"No, I'm sorry, not so far. Mrs. Sendall would know at once, of course."

"Yes, so she would." He paused. "I wondered if I could talk to the boy?"

"To Ben?"

"If that's his name."

Ginny swallowed. "That's rather awkward. I haven't told him anything, you see. He slept through it all. He heard nothing. He doesn't know there's been a burglary. I told him Mrs. Sendall had gone to stay with a friend."

"I see."

"To explain her absence."

"I understand that."

"So I'd rather you didn't talk to him if it could be avoided."

"If he didn't hear anything—"

"He didn't wake up."

"He might have seen or heard something immediately prior."

"Prior to the break-in, you mean?" Ginny said.

"Yes."

"I'd rather you didn't ask him," she repeated. "I'm sure he'd tell me if he had. And I'd tell you at once."

The sergeant sighed. He rubbed at the frown marks on his forehead. "As long as you can be quite sure he slept right through it all—"

"Yes, I can. Thank you, Sergeant. It would upset him dreadfully if we had to tell him. Not the burglary so much as Mrs. Sendall being hurt. They're great friends."

"If Mrs. Sendall doesn't recover—" He let the sentence trail away.

"If she doesn't recover," Ginny said, "that would be different."

The sergeant was at the door ready to go when she remembered Tom's remark.

"Did you ever meet my husband?" she asked. "John Benson."

She told him what Tom had said about John's visit to the police station.

"He came to see me," the sergeant said. There was no hesitation on his part in remembering. That seemed surprising to Ginny.

"What was it about?" she asked.

The sergeant sighed again, gently. "I don't know, Mrs. Benson. I was out, and he wouldn't tell the man on the desk. He made an appointment to see me, but he was killed before he could keep it."

Ginny sat down on the arm of a chair. "I have met you before, haven't I?" she said. "Your face is familiar."

"I came to see you at your house after the accident," he said. "I thought you might know what it was your husband had wanted to see me about." He regarded her with the same patient expression Ben sometimes adopted in their conversations together.

"I remember," Ginny said. "I remember you coming. But it was all blurred in my mind. They give you so many sedatives."

"And you still don't remember why your husband made that appointment?"

"No."

"I thought that might be why you mentioned Mr. Benson to me just now."

"No, I thought you could help me. I don't know what it was about. I've never known. He didn't tell me. I don't think I would have forgotten. Unless it was something small, like parking regulations or advice for making the house safe from burglars or something like that."

He smiled. He had a reassuring, fatherly smile for one so young. "I expect it was something like that. I wouldn't worry about it. Not at this late stage."

"There's no point, is there?" said Ginny. Her face was, for a moment, as desolate as her voice.

"Where is the boy?" the sergeant asked.

"In the garden somewhere. Why?"

"If he's seen me and asks, you'd better say I was selling insurance or encyclopedias."

Ginny smiled. "You're being very kind. Would you like a cup of tea or coffee? I'd do as much for any insurance man."

"No, thank you, Mrs. Benson." He shook hands in an oddly formal gesture. "I hope the old lady gets better."

She saw him out and went to ring the hospital again.

"It's a little early yet for news," she was told. "I should wait until this evening if I were you." The day seemed to have been going on forever, but it was only eleven.

She had no sooner put the phone down than it rang. This time it was Robert. He was coming at one, he announced, to take them out to lunch, Ben and her.

"I don't like to think of you alone in that house," he said. "How are you?"

"I'm fine, thank you, Robert. Don't worry about me."

"Any news of Mrs. Sendall?"

"Not yet. They said to try this evening. I don't know if that means they think she might recover consciousness by then. You know what hospitals are; they tell you nothing."

"And how's Ben?"

"He heard nothing at all. It's lucky, isn't it? I was afraid—"

"Afraid of what?"

"I don't know. That whoever attacked Mrs. Sendall

might think he had a witness. She's badly hurt. If she doesn't recover, that's murder, isn't it?"

"I'll try to get there earlier than one," he said. "You need someone there. I've got to look after my family."

"We're not your family, Robert."

"Not yet," he said.

She went into the kitchen and made coffee. Standing at the stove, waiting for the water to boil, she could see Ben rooting around in the bushes far up the garden. Looking for Alice, she supposed. If the cat had been in the house last night, she must have been terrified by what had gone on. Had she run away in fright? Or had they carelessly got rid of her? Oh, I hope they haven't killed her! she thought fervently. The atmosphere of violence seemed to penetrate the house in spite of all her efforts, like an invisible, poisonous mist, contaminating the air.

She poured out the coffee and sat down at the table to drink it, clutching the cup with both hands as if she were cold and it a winter not a summer day. The house, without Mrs. Sendall's cheerful voice and busy footsteps, seemed so empty, so silent. She found herself listening to the silence. She was trembling. You are an idiot, she told herself. The menace was gone. All the fears of the past days and weeks had reached their culmination last night. The game of statues was finished. It was all over. No one was going to return to this house. There would be no more intruders, no more violence. Then why was she trembling; why was she mortally afraid? It's the reaction, she explained to herself, and heard the quiet sound of a key turning in the front door lock.

She ran out into the hall. She called, "Mrs. Sendall!" though she knew it could not be she. She knew who it must be.

"Hello, Ginny," said James.

He had a small overnight bag with him which he had dropped on to the hall bench. He was returning a bunch of keys to his pocket.

"How did you get in?" Ginny said.

He raised an eyebrow at the gratuitous question. "With my key."

"Not your key."

"If you want to be pedantic, Mrs. Sendall's key. She lent me a spare."

"Or did you steal it from her bag? After you nearly murdered her? Why have you come back? Didn't you find what you were after? Did you think we'd be gone, Ben and me?"

She couldn't stop herself. The accusations burst out of her. Dangerous, dangerous, her brain sang, but she couldn't stop. His face was tight-lipped and grim. He turned away without speaking and went into the living room. She followed him.

"She's not dead. She's not recovered consciousness yet, but I understand she has a good chance." He spoke in a matter-of-fact way, like a commentator giving the racing results. He looked steadily at Ginny. "You think I attacked her."

"We know you're not her nephew. Her nephew's in Canada."

He suddenly shouted. "What the hell has that got to do with it?"

She realized he was possessed by anger, cold, raging anger that he was barely in control of. Her knees went weak. She sat down with a thud on the sofa. After a moment, James sat down wearily on the chair opposite.

"Who are you, James?" she whispered.

"I'm a friend of the family."

"How can I believe that?"

"You can believe what you like," he said quietly. "How much damage did they do?"

"Nothing lasting. I've cleared it up."

"Where's Ben?"

"He's all right. He's in the garden. We think Mrs. Sendall gave him a sleeping pill."

"What a marvelous woman!" He shook his head. "Where were you?"

"I was out with Robert Travis. He was telling me about you. He was the one who found you out."

"Clever Mr. Travis."

"Where were you last night, James?"

"Not back here beating up old ladies, as you so fondly imagine."

"The police will want to see you."

"I want to see them. I am on my way to see them, as it happens. I called in here to leave my bag and see if you were all right."

"In that order of importance?"

"What do you want me to say to that, Ginny?"

She shrugged. "I don't know. Do I still call you James?"

"As it happens, that part of the name is correct."

"But it's not Aldous?"

"No, it's not Aldous." He reached across the gap between them and took her hand. "Ginny, how much can I trust you?"

"You trust *me!"*

"You must remember all this began after you came here."

She was almost too indignant to speak. "It did not. It began a long time ago. Mrs. Sendall called the police in once because men were coming into her garden. You know that's so."

"Ah, but that was different. I've found the answer to that one. That was, as we all knew or suspected, Morgan."

"It was no secret. He wants this house. Mrs. Sendall told me. He told me himself."

"Yes, but now I know why. I've been talking to him this morning. He was the one who told me what had happened here."

"Then tell me. Why does he want the house?"

"He is going to build a marina."

It was so entirely different from what Ginny had expected, so normal and businesslike compared with all that imagination had aroused and the past night fulfilled that she did not at first take it in. It was too much of an anticlimax.

"A marina?" she repeated.

"Yes, you know, lots of berths for lots of boats. It's an interesting idea. It could be enormously successful. He thinks so. Local boy brings fame and prosperity to hometown. That's more or less how he put it. He's very devoted to his hometown."

"I can imagine him saying so," Ginny agreed. She wasn't sure if James was serious. She tried to think of Morgan in the role of public benefactor. It was hard to imagine, and yet hadn't he tried to give her money when he thought her so desperate as to attempt suicide? Wasn't that the act of a kind man, a man of generosity and goodwill?

"Where is the marina going to be?" she asked.

"Where the boatyard is at present. This is the nucleus. That's why he bought it, to get the water frontage. He has bought more land along the creek, he tells me. And then, Ginny, if you draw a straight line away from the boatyard, what do you come to?"

"The allotments," she said.

"And then?"

"Mrs. Sendall's house."

"Exactly."

"But a marina wouldn't stretch that far, would it?"

"Oh, it's a very ambitious project. This house would become the site of a huge hotel. The plan spreads over the entire area. To achieve his dream, as he calls it, he needs her land and the allotment land."

"Will he get it?"

"Very probably. When it's put up for sale, he'll make

the biggest bid, and I doubt if anyone will have a more
acceptable scheme for development to offer. I should
think the council would jump at it."

"Won't it cost a lot of money?"

"A great deal of money. That's how I got him to con-
firm my suspicions, by walking into his office and asking
him point-blank if he needed additional capital to finance
his marina scheme. It's the first time I've seen that man
look surprised. His mouth literally fell open in astonishment. When he recovered his voice, he bombarded me
with questions. How did I know? Who else knew? Where
had I heard? Who was I working for? I told him I'd put
two and two together from facts that were openly known
and that I was working for myself. I must say he seemed
pleased at any rate to have me pigeonholed at last, as he
put it. He'd been wondering what I was doing here, since
he knew I couldn't possibly be who I said I was. That was
interesting, don't you think, Ginny?"

"So that's what all this mystery and fuss have been
about."

"His one ambition, he said, ever since he came back
here for good has been to do something like this. To
change the life of the town. He's finding the finance himself, and he's going to stay in control. And if it all works
out as he hopes, he'll be on his way to being another
property tycoon, and then the sky's the limit. Europe,
America, you can see his empire in his eyes. A very en-
thusiastic gentleman underneath that suave exterior. He
doesn't change basically, though. It wasn't until he was
showing me out that he thought of telling me about Mrs.
Sendall."

"And there's nothing illegal about all this? He's done
nothing wrong?"

"I don't think so. He isn't even on the council any
more. He resigned a few months ago, he said, owing to
pressure of work, but I would imagine the real reason was

so that no one could say he was taking advantage of prior knowledge."

"And has he been?"

"Not really. Only so far as to discover that the allotments were going to be sold off as soon as they'd found alternative land for the allotment holders. And that the possibility of building a marina had been discussed once again by the council and discarded as being too expensive. It's a project that's been on and off again for years. But both these are things anyone could pick up. I found them out easily enough. There's nothing secret about them. The only thing that is secret is his scheme. He's asked me to keep quiet about it until the allotments are definitely up for sale. He doesn't want anyone coming in and shooting the price up. He's resigned to paying more for Mrs. Sendall's property than he wanted to or even waiting, as he put it bluntly, until she's dead."

"But he wouldn't kill her deliberately, would he?"

He shook his head. "A bit of pressure. Tramps in the garden. Even then she frightened him off by calling in the police that first time. I asked him outright today. He told me he'd done nothing these past weeks beyond asking Mrs. Sendall once more if she would be prepared to sell."

"I'm surprised," Ginny said.

"You sound almost disappointed."

"I don't know. I began by believing him genuine, but then things Mrs. Sendall said and the strange atmosphere there's been—it's terrible, isn't it, what imagination does to you?" She tried to smile. "I seem to get frightened very easily these days. When I went with Ben on that picnic, I thought I'd lost him and I became hysterical. But there was nothing wrong. I suppose I must have become a very neurotic woman. I don't want to be, but you can't always help yourself."

"You're not neurotic," James said. "Though you have acquired that reputation."

She raised her head and met his eyes. "Because of the gassing?"

He nodded.

"That wasn't attempted suicide, James. You must believe me. It was an accident."

"I don't think it was an accident. I think someone wanted to kill you."

She said, after a pause, "I sympathize with Morgan. You have a habit of shocking people into silence."

"I'm sorry, Ginny."

"But *why?*"

"I don't know."

"And who? And who broke in here last night? The same people? Were they after me, then, not Mrs. Sendall? James, I'm trembling again. I'm such a coward." All those unseen hands stretching out behind you. The game wasn't over. The faceless statues were still waiting.

James got up and poured her out some gin barely diluted with water.

"It should be Dutch gin for Dutch courage," Ginny remarked.

"Drink it up anyway, and don't choke."

She drank it down. The spirit warmed her.

"It'll give me indigestion," she said. "It always does this time of day."

He sat beside her, quietly waiting, quietly watching.

"Mrs. Sendall might know who attacked her," she said. "She might recover consciousness anytime."

"I'm going to the hospital after I've been to the police," James said. "I want to make quite sure that steps are being taken to counter the possibility that someone might try to prevent her recovering for that very reason."

Ginny didn't point out that the police might not let him leave. She said, "Surely they wouldn't murder her!"

"It depends what they're after. They might want to try again later if they missed it this time."

"You've no idea if Mrs. Sendall has anything enormously valuable in the house?" Ginny said. "Something out of the ordinary?"

"I think she would have told us."

She noticed how it had become "us." He had put himself on the side of the angels, but she had no more reason to trust him now than she had when he walked in. Could the anger have been because he had not found what he wanted last night? Because Mrs. Sendall was still alive? Or because he had struck down the wrong person? How did she know he would go to the police? How did she know he wouldn't go straight to the hosiptal and for the very reason he had given her, to silence Mrs. Sendall?

"If it's not Morgan," she said, and only just prevented herself from saying, if it's not you, "then who is it? Who is responsible?"

"There is another actor on the scene," James said. "There is Robert Travis."

She stared. "You can't be serious."

"Why not?"

"Well, he's no connection with anything."

"He's connected with the bookshop."

"And what has that to do with the break-in?"

"Bear with me, Ginny. I don't know what the link is any more than you do or if there is one even. But I do know one fact you don't which I'll tell you in a minute. So you tell me first what you know about Travis."

"Not an awful lot," she said frankly. "He comes from London. He's worked in bookshops and wants to own one eventually. He came into some money a few months ago, and that's why he's down here and why he's thinking of taking on the shop."

"Why here? Why this particular shop?"

"Perhaps he'd heard it was cheap."

"How did he hear? It's not on the agent's list of vacant property. We know that."

"Maybe Morgan told him."

"You think he knew Morgan before he came here?"

"He might have done. But perhaps someone in the book trade told him. They must have their own network of information. All professions do, don't they?"

"Yes, that's possible."

"And there's another thing," she said. "He was with me last night. He couldn't have been the man who attacked Mrs. Sendall. And if, as you say, that accident with the gas wasn't an accident, it couldn't have been Robert either. He'd taken Mrs. Sendall and Ben on a picnic."

But it could have been you, James, she thought. No one knows where you were at either time.

"You make a good advocate for him, Ginny, I'm sorry to say. I'm only interested, you see, because of that fact I mentioned. I have found out where the previous tenant is now. The one who went bust. He's in prison."

"Good heavens. What for?"

"Posssessing stolen property. Not here. London. And the name he used here, Charles Mayhew, is only one of several he's known by."

"How on earth did you find that out?"

"Friends of friends."

"No wonder Morgan has been so cagey about the shop. It wouldn't have been good publicity for his agency— would it?—if it got about that he had crooks as tenants. Anyway, if you wait, you can ask Robert all your questions himself. He's coming here at one to take us to lunch—"

She broke off, forgetting what else she had been about to say. She was conscious of an odd sensation. Her mind felt confused. A pattern was emerging, fragmentary, elusive. Memories were painfully stirring, like a numbed limb pricking and aching back to life.

"Did you know," she said slowly, "that my husband made an appointment with the police just before he was killed? He died before he could keep it, and no one knew what he had wanted to see them about."

"The bookshop," James said. "You think it was something he had found out about the bookshop?"

"John said Mayhew knew nothing about books, and now you say he was a criminal, arrested for possessing stolen property. John went to the shop quite a few times. I'm wondering if he saw stolen property there. Could that be it? Or perhaps it was something else that puzzled him, something he thought he ought to talk to someone knowledgeable about. But before he could speak to the police, before he could tell anyone his suspicions, he died."

She stopped abruptly. She was staring into space, pale as a ghost.

"What is it?" James held her hand tightly. "What's the matter?"

"I've remembered. I've remembered the end of my dream. What he said. What he said just before the car crashed. He said, 'The steering's gone, Ginny.' That's what he said. 'The steering's gone.' "

Her hand clung to his. "It wasn't us, you see; it was the car. And the car should have been all right—shouldn't it? —because it had just been overhauled. So why should the steering go?" She turned great stricken eyes on James. "So you see what it means? It wasn't an accident, don't you see, James? It couldn't have been. Someone must have damaged the steering mechanism. They must have done it deliberately. It was murder, James. Murder."

❧ 7 ❧

THE WORRYING THING to Ginny about James' reaction was his stillness. At the word "murder" he went as quiet and motionless as a cat watching a bird. He watched Ginny. She stumbled on, struggling to express to him her sudden overwhelming conviction that the accident which had haunted her so long had been deliberately caused.

"That was why I kept dreaming about it, don't you see? I knew something was wrong. I thought it was my own sense of guilt that wouldn't let it rest, but it wasn't that. It was the knowledge that it wasn't, couldn't have been an accident." With every word she spoke she became more certain.

"I disagree," James said. "It could have been an accident. It could easily have been a fault the garage overlooked. I don't share your faith in the thoroughness of that overhaul the car had had."

"But the steering!" she protested. "How could a fault there be overlooked?"

"By not specifically looking for it," he said. "And even if they did check, there might have been nothing to see at that stage. Nuts work loose; things snap. Accidents happen."

Ginny sighed heavily and rested her face in her hands. "Who do you think was responsible?" James persisted. "Mayhew? Robert Travis? Even I have to admit that Travis, to whom I happen to have taken a dislike for purely personal and amorous reasons, wasn't even here at the time. And when and where do you suppose Mayhew could have got at the car?"

"It would be left parked in the street while John saw booksellers."

"The streets where bookshops are are usually a bit too public for hanky-panky with a saw or whatever."

"It could have been in a side street or a car park."

"Don't forget the car would have been carefully examined after the crash. The investigators would have found anything deliberately cut or broken."

"In the state it was in?" Ginny said. "You didn't see it."

"I think so," he said. "Even in the state it must have been in. Where is it now, do you know?"

"It was scrapped," Ginny said. "It was beyond repair."

James stood up. She got the impression he was about to leave.

"I don't understand you," she said. "You seemed to be hinting so many sinister things about that bookshop."

"Forget it," he said. "There's no connection. Though your husband may have suspected that Mayhew was something more than an incompetent bookseller and wanted to talk to the police about his suspicions, his death can have been nothing more than a coincidence." He stooped and picked up her glass. "I'll get you another drink."

"I don't want one." But she sipped it when he brought it, and she noticed that this time he had made himself a drink too. When the phone rang, she half got up, but James was before her. She heard the murmur of his voice in the hall, too low for her to catch the sense of the words. He rang off and came back into the living room. He finished his drink with one gulp and put the empty glass down on the table.

"I've got to go," he said. "That was the police."

"Have they news of Mrs. Sendall?"

"No. They want to see me. They'd heard I was back. I suppose Morgan told them."

"James, you do know they may arrest you?"

"On what charge?"

She looked at him helplessly. "Don't be silly. All this. The burglary. Everything."

He smiled, the boyishly charming smile of their earlier meetings. "There's no proof, Ginny. That's what I've been trying to tell you. There's no proof. Against anybody. So don't mention your suspicions to anyone, anyone at all." He paused. "I'd be glad if you took that as a warning."

"A warning from an anonymous well-wisher? Isn't that what they put in threatening letters?"

"Just as long as you heed it," James said. "you can think of it as you will."

Ben was in a state of mind unusual for him; he was both bored and uneasy. He was bored with his search for Alice and uneasy at Mrs. Sendall's absence.

He had hunted Alice all morning throughout the garden, among the thickest bushes, along the open pathways and the crumbling walls, and in the branches of every tree. He had covered the front garden, as well as the grounds at the back, stalking his way along the curving drive and even making a quick reconnaissance along the road in case she had been hurt by a car during the night and had crawled into the gutter. It wasn't likely. Her world extended from the back of the house toward the creek. He had seldom seen her in the front garden, which was a gloomy sort of spot with too many rhododendron bushes, but even cats did unexpected things. Everybody did. Like Mrs. Sendall going off without saying good-bye. Could she possibly have forgotten about last night? She must have, or she wouldn't have gone without saying something. He didn't like people going away suddenly. Sometimes they didn't come back. His father had gone away and never came back.

From his position now, at the near end of the tennis court, he heard the sound of a car driving off. There had been another car earlier. From his lookout by the front gate he had seen it drive past, a man who was a stranger to him at the wheel. By the time he had worked his way up to the house, the man had driven away again. This second car might be more interesting; it might have brought Mrs. Sendall back. It might have been a taxi. He got up, tired of stalking, and went up to the house. Through the living-room window he saw his mother walking up and down, up and down, her arms clutched about her. He remembered her walking like that, silently pacing up and down, in the old house. The sight worried him. He began to back away. The car couldn't have been bringing Mrs. Sendall home. She would have been in the room talking to his mother.

He walked disconsolately down the garden toward the gate in the wall. He opened it and stood looking across the allotments at the outline of the church. The church didn't frighten him anymore. Not really frighten. Last night had cured him. They had taken the torch and gone out together to play the game. Then they had come home, and he had had hot milk and gone to bed, expecting to finish the game in the morning. That was what Mrs. Sendall had said. She'd said it was too late to go on that night. He knew the church, but she didn't. She'd need lots of daylight, and it was already quite dark inside. It wasn't like her to forget, but she must have forgotten about it when she woke up this morning because of her friend's being ill. It had been exciting going there so late. He wouldn't have gone on his own, but it had been all right with a friend. Mrs. Sendall had said the tramp wouldn't be in there, and he hadn't been. And if he weren't there at night, he wouldn't be there in daylight. So it was all right. He made up his mind and set off for the church.

He still went carefully, out of habit, when he got near, scouting right around the outside of the building before returning to the side door with its broken planks and its dark jagged entrance beckoning into the interior. He ducked his head and stepped inside, and the familiar smell of rotting wood and decaying plaster surged to meet him.

Last night Mrs. Sendall had waited outside this door while Ben plunged within, torch held in rigid hand, neck prickling with an almost enjoyable alarm, moving into the shadows with the knowledge that nothing could harm him, because Mrs. Sendall was within call and ghosts and horrors do not trouble adults. Even so, he had been in and out again in two minutes. He had not been frightened, but there was no point in running unnecessary risks.

Now he was pleased to find he felt as happy and confident within the confines of the church as he had been in the old days before the tramp appeared. He scuffed his feet triumphantly through the debris strewn across the floor, stretched his arms out wide and sent a proprietorial "coo-ee" up to the echoing roof where soaring hymns of praise had once resounded richly back on the heads of the devout below. His paean of rejoicing resulted now only in a scattered fall of plaster. He walked around the church on a ceremonial tour and climbed the swaying wooden staircase to the gallery. He took the right-hand stairs. The left-hand staircase was full of rotten steps, just as the left-hand pillars of the single elegant row which supported the gallery seemed more eaten with rot than the right. In the gallery he sat in his accustomed place on the pew for a moment for old times' sake and looked through the window, his long-established spyhole, for the same reason. No one was about. All was clear. He felt like a general returning to a victorious battlefield as he descended the stairs again, much pleased with his bravado. Below, the pulpit awaited him, with the steps leading into that tiny circular space from which the tramp had risen up and seized him. Ben had mounted the first step, his hand resting on the heavy round head of the baluster, when he heard a faint rustling movement. It came from within the pulpit.

He froze, unable to move. He shut his eyes, and he could see in his mind the hand that grasped his and the thin body tumbling down the steps and the dead face staring at him from the barge. He would have run for his life if he had not been paralyzed with the fear. The rustling came again, and then a stranger noise sounded, like a cry, faint and lost like a bird's thin mew heard from far away. He opened his eyes. Thin little mewing noises. He leaped up the stairs to the pulpit and stood gazing down, gulping with relief and delight.

"Alice!"

Alice lay curled up on a bed of torn newspapers and old rags which the tramp had abandoned there and lazily suckled her kittens. Three tabby kittens and one black groped blindly and protestingly for her teats and fell into the silence of satisfied greed as they found them. Alice raised her head, blinked her soft eyes at Ben, and began to purr.

He squatted down on his heels beside her. "Alice!" He was speechless with pleasure. He stroked her head and touched her kittens with his forefinger.

"So this is where you were," he said. "I've been looking for you all over the place." Alice shifted her position slightly, stretching out a paw, and one kitten fell, toppling over the others. They became confused and began crawling over each other, nuzzling and mewing. Alice yawned.

"You must be hungry," Ben said. "I'll get your dinner and bring it here. And milk."

He stood up and so witnessed the entry of another visitor to the church.

"Hello," he said cheerfully. "I didn't know you were back. Mum said you'd gone to London."

"So I had," said the newcomer. "I've come back."

"Come up here, come and see what I've found. Alice has had her kittens. Four of them."

His friend joined him on the steps.

"Very pretty," he said.

"Cats make very good mothers. She's been looking for a place to have them for days, Mrs. Sendall said. She was afraid she'd have them in her wardrobe. She did once before, she said."

"I've been looking for you, Ben."

"Have you? I think you'd better step back a bit. She doesn't like us getting too close. It's all right, Alice." Alice had half raised herself, the kittens dragging at her fur. She watched the man and the boy warily.

"You come here a lot, don't you, Ben?"

"I have been, quite a lot."

"You found something here once, didn't you?"

"I find lots of things."

"And you keep them."

"They're treasure trove," Ben explained.

The man nodded. "Usually when you find treasure trove, you can keep it, but not this time. You see, what you found belongs to me, and I'm afraid you must give them back to me. But I tell you what I'll do. I'll pay you a penny for each one."

Ben couldn't think what he was getting at. Why should anything of his be left in the church? And why, once thrown away, should he want them back?

"You don't mean the cigarettes, do you?" he asked. "Because I lost one of those."

"No, I don't mean cigarettes. I mean diamonds. Do you know what diamonds are, Ben?"

Ben laughed. "I haven't got any diamonds."

"Oh, yes, you have. It must have been you. We watched to see who came here, and it was only you and that tramp, and the tramp didn't have them. We made sure of that."

It was at that point that Ben began to feel alarmed. It was the change in manner and in voice, the sense of urgency, the hard pressure of the man's hand as he grasped Ben's arm and turned him to face him.

"Where are they hidden, Ben?"

"I didn't find any diamonds," Ben repeated. "I know what diamonds are. My mother's got diamonds in her ring. I didn't find anything like that."

"They are uncut diamonds, eight of them. They wouldn't look shiny and bright; they'd look dull, like chunks of pond ice."

"Like pebbles?"

"That's right, like pebbles." He drew in his breath. "So you did find them."

"I found some pebbles."

"And you kept them."

"I haven't got them." His voice came out like a squeak. He tried to move away, but the man held him. Behind them Alice stirred uneasily.

"They're not in the house. We've searched every inch of that house. You gave them to your mother, didn't you? And she's put them in a safe place." He looked at Ben's face and tried to soften his voice. "She doesn't realize that I am the owner; otherwise, she'd give them back straight away. Just tell me where she's put them, Ben, that's all. She hasn't been away. She wouldn't dare to leave them in the shop. They must be in the house or near the house, so where are they, Ben, where are they?"

Bewildered, confused, frightened, Ben opened his mouth. His shout of defiance came out as a thin, reedy cry. "Why don't you ask her?"

He stepped back. The man followed. His feet, so much larger than Ben's, trod on the kitten Ben had missed. The kitten squealed in pain, and Alice, rising to the defense of her young, struck out with angry paw and clawed the man in the ankle. He swore and stooped to brush her off, and Ben broke free and vaulted over the banister rail to the floor.

He darted to the door. When he couldn't see it, he panicked. Then he realized the light from outside was blocked by the figure of another man standing before the entrance. This second man came after him. Ben turned and streaked for the gallery. The first man was down from the pulpit. The two men paused and spoke to each other. In the right-hand gallery Ben was trying desperately to break the cracked window. Glass fell in spiky shards, but not enough for him to cram his body through the gap, and even if he managed, it, he thought wildly, where could he go? He would fall and kill himself. He dropped behind a pew and waited. They were coming, one up the left-hand staircase, the other up the right. Ben wriggled his way as fast as long practice and panic allowed to the center of the gallery where the organ had been and where there was still projecting masonry to make cover. From his place of concealment he listened to the two men shouting to each other as they searched each wing of the gallery. They made a lot of noise overturning the bits of wood, the boxes and odd chairs and discarded junk. Dust and plaster rose in clouds. The building itself seemed to creak and stir. They were converging on him. The one on the left was not as methodical as the one on the right. He had almost got to the center gallery. The other was farther away. Ben grasped a torn piece of wooden paneling that lay near him and tried the trick he had seen so many times on television. He flung the wood as far as he could to the right. It made a satisfying clatter against the pew. The second man ran toward it. As he passed him, Ben got up and dashed for the left-hand stairs. The men saw and pursued him. His heart pounding, he half slid, half fell across the gallery. He sensed rather than saw the hands reaching to grab him and took a flying jump down the stairs. The step he landed on was rotten. It broke away under him and sent him crashing down the length of the staircase to lie limply on the floor beneath, with all the wind and sense knocked out of him.

Alice was a prudent and sensible cat. She waited, crouched well down, ears pressed back, the kittens guarded but ignored, until quiet was restored to the church. She then waited for a further period of time before so much as venturing a sensitive nose out of the pulpit. When the silence remained undisturbed, she padded stealthily down the stairs. She paused at the base, sniffing and watching. Satisfied, she moved across the floor and out of the door into the open air. She stood there, considering her further action. The safe birthplace was safe no longer. She had no choice but to move, and the first place that might be considered secure was within the garden wall of her own house. It was a long and hard task that she set herself, but there was no alternative. She went back to her kittens. She licked them all over, then grasping one at random in her mouth, set off again down the stairs.

At quarter to one Ginny came out into the garden to look for Ben.

She hadn't realized how late it was. Ever since James had left, she had been wandering aimlessly about the house, her mind in a turmoil of uncertainty. There was no proof, James had said, and he was right. But mightn't proof be found? Mightn't evidence be uncovered if only one knew the right way to go about it?

She rang the police station and asked for the sergeant; but it was a different man who came to the phone, and she could not ask for the right one because the sergeant had never given her his name.

"It's about the burglary at Mrs. Sendall's," she said. "He came to see me." She felt it was pointless to say it was really about the possibility of a car accident long settled up and written off in official files turning out to be a murder case after all. Any telephone message she left trying to express that thought would only muddle everyone up hopelessly, she was sure.

Detective Sergeant Wood was the officer she wanted, she was told, but he was out at present.

"Is a Mr. James Aldous there?" she asked. "He was coming to see Sergeant Wood."

"No, madam. There's no one of that name here."

"Mrs. Sendall's nephew?"

"No, he's not here either."

She gave up.

She changed from working clothes into a dress and was brushing her hair at the bedroom window when she became aware that Ben whom she'd been keeping an eye on on and off all morning, was no longer visible. Even when he was in hiding, it was usually possible to spot his whereabouts from the upper windows of the house, but nothing was stirring, no bushes quivering at his passing, no agitation of small birds. She opened the window and called him. There was no answering shout.

She put on her shoes and went to find him. After five minutes she was sure he was not in the garden. He was a cooperative boy. He usually came if you yelled long enough, even without Mrs. Sendall's useful whistle.

She went out of the gate into the allotments, wondering which direction to take. Would Ben have gone as far as the creek? After all, he didn't know Robert was coming to take them to lunch. She began to walk along the path which led, with many diversions around the plots of cultivated land, across the allotments and down to the towpath. Every now and then she stopped and called Ben's name. Her cries faded into the embracing stillness. It was an empty landscape of green summer lethargy, the only movement the hovering insects, the darting butterflies. Not quite the only movement. At a crossroad on the network of paths she met Alice, loping along with patient determination, a small dark object dangling from her mouth. Ginny thought at first she had caught a rat or a vole, until she got a clearer view.

"Alice!" she cried. "You've had your kittens. Where are they? Where are you taking them?" The interruption flustered Alice. Put out of her stride, with an obstacle in front, she stopped, hesitated, backed, turned, and trotted back toward the church. Ginny followed her.

She found the kittens, then left them well alone so that the now-distraught Alice would not be further upset. The cat dropped her load beside its mewling brethren, examined them carefully, washed them, and settled down to feed them, abandoning for the time being the move to safer walls.

Ginny inspected the church curiously. She hadn't been inside it before. She hadn't known it was possible to get inside. This was where the tramps must come for shelter. It was pretty decrepit. One staircase appeared on the point of collapse with gaping holes in the stairway and a broken handrail. The gleam of white at the foot of the stairs caught her glance, and she bent and picked up a fragment of coarse pottery. It had the remains of a blue pattern on it. It was like the odd pieces Ben collected. And so was this, that lay next to it, the lump of green bottle glass, and so was this, a matchbox, empty, she discovered, but still containing a bed of cotton wool such as might protect a larva.

She sat down on the steps, worried but not yet frightened. They were Ben's things. He had been here, but when? Today, yesterday, last week? Had he tired of these treasures, or had he accidentally dropped them while exploring the church? And then she noticed the torn strip of cloth on the rough edge of the rail. Blue cotton, like the shirt he was wearing today.

"Hello, Ginny." A man had entered and stood smiling at her.

"Robert! Where did you spring from?"

"I walked down from the house. I saw you come in here. It's taken me five minutes to find the way in. What on earth are you doing sitting there like a figure of doom?"

He kicked aside some rubbish at his feet and gazed around the interior. "An ecclesiastical slum. My God, it's a mess, isn't it?"

Ginny looked at him with affection. "I'm very glad to see you. I know it must be ages past one. I'm sorry I wasn't at the house. I was looking for Ben. I can't find him. I'm afraid something's happened to him."

"Nonsense," Robert said comfortingly. "Nothing happens to the Bens of this world. Why should you think that?"

"He's been here today, and he must have fallen on these stairs. Look, he tore his shirt here, and those are all things he carried in his pocket."

"If he'd hurt himself, he'd either go home for aid and succor or be lying in a heap where he fell. Since he's doing neither of these things, I should imagine he tore his shirt *en passant* without noticing. He does dash around a lot, doesn't he?"

"He was given a sleeping pill last night. It couldn't have any aftereffects, could it?"

Robert laughed. "Don't be silly." He held out his hand. "Come on, we'll go and look for him."

Ginny took his hand, and he pulled her to her feet. His arms came around her in a close embrace.

"That was very smooth," said Ginny.

He kissed her.

"And so was that. Let me get my breath. Robert, you're more pleased with yourself today than I've ever known you. You've even stopped apologizing."

"Well, why shouldn't I be pleased? My only rival is exposed as the villain he is and will soon be locked in the clink."

"They've arrested James? For the burglary?"

He shrugged. "I don't know. But they soon will. Who else could have done it?"

"A tramp," Ginny suggested weakly.

Robert didn't bother to reply.

Ginny remembered Alice. "The cat's had kittens. In here of all places. Come and look. They're tucked into the pulpit. Sweet little things."

Alice didn't welcome the intrusion. Her amber eyes were watchful, and her tail lashed from side to side.

"We shouldn't disturb her," Ginny said. "I'll come back and move her after lunch. I found her carrying one of the kittens across the allotments, so she doesn't mean to stay here and I don't want her getting lost."

Robert gazed up at the roof. "I think she's wise. From the state of this place, I should think the ceiling's going to come down at any minute. Aren't they supposed to put proper hoardings around unsafe buildings?"

"They boarded it up," Ginny pointed out.

"That wasn't very successful, was it? The whole world seems to have spent its time tracking in and out of here, you and Ben and the tramp and the cat. It's been more like Victoria Station than a condemned property. Now where shall we look for Ben? Didn't you tell me he spent a lot of time by the creek? We'll look there first."

It was pleasant, Ginny found, to be taken in hand by the newly dominant Robert. He waved away her idea of going back to the house first to see if Ben had returned there in her absence.

"One of us would have seen him," Robert said. "Or he would have heard you calling him. I heard you calling. That's how I knew where you were."

She accepted it. The worry was growing, but it was controllable. She was determined to make it stay that way. She wasn't going to get hysterical as she had on the day of the picnic. Ben had been all right then, and he would turn out to be all right now. It was merely a question of finding him.

They searched up and down the creek, among the broken sheds and the barges and the overgrown ditch that separated the allotments from the towpath, and along the wooden fencing that remained intact here and there. The tide had been high but was turning, the mud covered by dense gray water swirling to the pull of the current and lapping at the uneven banks. Ginny tried not to give in to her worst fear, that Ben had slipped on the edge of the bank and drowned in the muddy water. That thick ooze at the bottom of the creek would hold fast a man, let alone a small boy. He could never escape.

Robert came up to her where she stood staring into the water. He put his hand lightly on her shoulder.

"We haven't tried the boatyard yet," he said. "He might be inside." She nodded.

It was a hopeful sign, she thought, that the gate to the boatyard was open. At least, Ben could have got in there easily enough. At first sight the place seemed deserted. The workshop door was open; but no one was inside, and no one was working on any of the boats chocked up in the yard.

"Taylor!" Robert called. "Are you there?"

They were answered by the sound of tackle rattling across a deck. They walked over to the jetty, to the boat tied up there. Robert called again and the man sorting gear in the cockpit stood up and, resting his hands on the coaming, asked them what they wanted.

"You remember me, don't you?" Robert said. "I hired a boat from you for a picnic."

"Oh, yes," Taylor acknowledged. "Do you want to hire it again?"

"Not at the moment. Do you remember the boy who was with me? We're looking for him. He likes boats. We wondered if he'd been here."

Ginny had been gazing at the man, wondering why she should think she knew him. It came to her suddenly. The man at the water's edge, the day she thought she had lost Ben. Taylor had been the man who appeared as if out of nowhere, with grease-stained hands, the man whose boat had broken down.

"You do know him, Mr. Taylor," she said quickly. "He talked to you about your boat one afternoon out on the marshes. He's my son. I asked you if you'd seen him then. Don't you recall it?"

Taylor shifted his eyes to her. He had an intent, unsmiling glance that she found disconcerting. He studied her closely, but the main impression he gave her was one of indifference. She had not thought much about him the first time she had seen him; now she decided she didn't like him.

"I remember the boy," he said.

"Has he been here today?"

He shook his head.

"You haven't seen him at all? Playing on the bank perhaps?"

"I didn't say I hadn't seen him," Taylor replied. "I said he hadn't been here."

"You have seen him then?" He didn't reply. He looked impassively from her to Robert. Ginny turned to Robert in exasperation.

"What's the matter with him?" she whispered. "Isn't he all there?"

Robert raised his voice. "Where did you see the boy?"

Taylor jerked his thumb. "Back there away, running along the embankment."

"The embankment only starts at the river!" Ginny cried. "You must be mistaken. He wouldn't have gone so far."

Taylor shrugged. "Well, that's where I saw him. Running hard. Running away from home, maybe. Boys do, don't they?"

"Of course he's not running away," Ginny said indignantly. "He must be lost. Robert, we've got to get after him."

Taylor straightened up. He said casually, "Want me to take you there?"

She wasn't sure what he meant.

"Guide us to the place in your car, does he mean?" she asked Robert.

"Take us in his boat, I think," Robert said. "Anyway, I haven't got the car today. I came to the house by bus." He looked at her. "It'd take us a long time to catch Ben up, walking."

"Lots of treacherous dikes down that way," Taylor said. "And deep water."

"How far is he, exactly?" Ginny asked him.

Taylor considered. "Near where I saw you that time. Where the boat broke down."

"As far as that!" How long had he been gone, she thought, to get as far away as that?

"It can't be Ben," she said to Robert. "It must be another boy."

"It was the same boy I saw that day," Taylor said. "Still"—he turned away—"it's all one to me."

"Robert—" She appealed to him. "What shall we do?"

"Accept Mr. Taylor's kind offer," Robert said. "It's the quickest way to get there."

Taylor's boat was a thirty-two-foot motor cruiser powered by twin diesels which gave her a top speed of around eighteen knots. It was a good working seaboat with nothing pretentious about it, but to Ginny's inexperienced eye, it looked like an exceptionally racy and powerful sort of craft to find moored in a quiet creek. However, you needed the power if you wanted to keep to a schedule at sea, Robert assured her, and Taylor's clients most likely did. He had to be able to bring them back at the times they wanted. The cruiser also had an extremely large cockpit which made it particularly suitable for the paid fishing parties Taylor took out.

"Have you been fishing in her?" Ginny asked Robert.

He shook his head. "This is the first time I've been on this boat. I must say she handles well."

Taylor had switched on the engines and let them idle in neutral while they cast off from the mooring. Now he eased the boat away from the bank and out into the central channel, keeping both throttles down low until they were well away.

"You better keep a sharp lookout," he called. "He might have started back." He grinned. "If he's not running away from home, that is."

Ginny leaned against the side of the cockpit and said quietly to Robert, "I can't stand that man. I'm sure it must be the wrong boy."

"Well, even if it was, we get the best view of the bank from here," Robert pointed out. "If Ben is anywhere between here and the river, we should spot him."

They moved gently downstream, following the curves of the creek as it bent its way through the open country toward the river. Ginny gazed at the monotonous landscape of bank and field and scattered trees until her eyes ached. She was filled with sick uncertainty about the wisdom of their actions. She was fearful that somehow she had missed Ben and that he had gone back home on his own and was now sitting there alone, waiting for her in that perhaps still-threatened house.

She said to Robert, "Let's get Taylor to put us off anywhere here. It's a wild-goose chase, I know it is. Ben would never have got so far in the time. He's only eight. It would take a grown man longer."

"When did you last see him?"

"I don't know. About half past eleven."

He looked at his watch. "He could have got a fair way, Ginny. I think we might as well go on now we've started."

"No," she insisted. "No. I want to get off. We can search on our own, Robert, just as well."

"All right." He went over to Taylor at the wheel. Ginny couldn't hear what they were saying. The noise of the engines made it impossible to hear from a distance anything spoken quietly. That was another reason for leaving, she thought. If Ben were out here, if he were calling for help, surely with all this roaring, she might easily miss his shouts?

Taylor was looking at his watch and pointing ahead. Robert came back.

"Well?"

"He can't stop along this stretch. There are mudbanks. He has to stick to the channel. He could get stranded if he goes into the bank."

"But it's high tide," Ginny said. "There's plenty of water now, isn't there?"

"Not near the banks, apparently, not for a boat this size. He'll put us off further up if we want." He was concerned for her. "Is that all right, Ginny?"

"It will have to be, won't it? We can't ask him to risk his boat. But, oh, Robert, I wish we hadn't come. We're so tied now. We've lost our freedom of action."

"We'll find Ben," Robert said. "Don't worry." He went back to stand beside Taylor.

Suppose it was true, Ginny wondered. Suppose Ben had been running away, just as Taylor said. He might have seen or heard something last night, before the sleeping pill took effect, and only remembered during the morning. He might have completely forgotten it or known it only as a vague dream, until something happened to nudge his memory. He would worry then because Ginny had said nothing to him about it. He would worry about Mrs. Sendall; he might be frightened about what would happen to him. He might even have seen the actual man who had attacked Mrs. Sendall. He might have recognized him.

He had been happy and carefree enough when he got up. What had happened during the morning to change the situation? She tried to think, to put events into consecutive order. Eileen and Tom had come to the house. So had the detective sergeant. So had James.

Now she wanted to hurry to the creek where she and Ben had picnicked that thundery afternoon. Now she could nearly believe that Ben had run there to hide, thinking that no one would believe or protect him, especially his mother. It would seem to him, having wakened to the tidy house, the normal breakfast, that no one realized anything evil had happened in the night. Why had she had to lie to him? She should have told him the truth, about Mrs. Sendall, about everything. Her efforts to protect him were only endangering him the more.

They had reached the river and the embankment that ran the length of it to the sea. Nothing moved along the towpath; no figure of a small boy was silhouetted against the skyline. She became aware of Robert back at her side.

He smiled at her reassuringly. "I think there'll be a place soon where it'll be safe for him to put us off."

"I don't want to stop now," she said. "I want him to go on, as fast as he can. Please tell him. Robert, what's he doing?"

Taylor was beckoning Robert and, when he went over to him, obviously asked him to take the wheel. As Ginny crossed the cockpit, Taylor was disappearing down the companionway.

"Where's he gone?" Ginny's anxiety was taking the form of a vast impatience to get this journey over. Taylor knew his boat and every inch of the river. Robert would have to go cautiously.

"It's late," Robert pointed out. "He says he hasn't eaten. He's gone down to get something."

They already seemed to Ginny to be moving more slowly. Robert had throttled back the engines.

"No, he must stay," she said. "He knows the river. He's got to stay at the wheel. I'll tell him. I can easily get him something to eat."

"Ginny—" Robert protested. But she was down the companionway and into the saloon before he could stop her.

It was a large saloon with a bunk on one side, a table and a bench seat that could be used as a second bunk on the other. There were the usual storage compartments and a galley immediately inside. Everything looked as if it had seen a good deal of wear. The bunk was covered with gear and odds and ends such as a thick sweater, an anorak, and an empty bottle of beer. A pair of sea boots had been tossed onto the other seat, together with a couple of shabby cushions and a blanket.

Taylor was standing at the far end, his hand on the bulkhead door which led to the forecabin.

"And what do you think you're doing?" he said.

"Mr. Travis said you wanted something to eat. I'll make something."

"Mr. Travis said that, did he?" he mocked. It seemed as if by moving around his boat, she had evoked his open hostility. But who asked them on it in the first place, she thought. Perhaps this occured to him too, for he added less roughly, "I've changed my mind. I'm not hungry." He looked at her, then shrugged. "You can make some tea, if you like."

Ginny said, "How far is it to the creek where you saw Ben?"

"Don't you know?"

He never gave a straight answer to any question.

"How can I know?" she said. "We went by bus before."

"Oh, that's how you got there? I wondered. It's not far.

I'll soon have you there." He pushed past her and vanished up the steps. She noticed as he passed that his clothes smelled of a mixture of fish and engine oil, and so did he.

She sighed. Having committed herself, she felt obliged to make tea. She turned to the galley. There was a whistling kettle, reasonably full of water. A plastic bowl in the sink contained two egg-encrusted plates, two knives and forks, and two dirty mugs. The teapot, thick with tea leaves, stood on the side. She managed to light the stove and set the kettle to boil. In a cupboard by the sink she found the tea caddy. There was no fresh milk, but there was an open tin of condensed milk with a yellow fall of cream congealed over the label.

She washed the dishes and stacked them on the draining board. Pulling open cupboards and drawers to find a third mug, she noticed thrust down the side of a drawer what looked like a white and red tea cloth. She took it out to dry the dishes only to discover that it was not cotton or linen but silk and that the red was not an edging but a curving pattern than ran all over the cloth. She was holding it in her hands when Robert came down to tell her they were entering the creek.

"Well, well," he said, "what have you got there?"

She spread it out for him to see. "A silk scarf. Isn't it pretty? Just the thing for a young girl of sixteen. Did your niece like it, Robert?"

He said nothing for a very long moment; then he said lightly, with the throwaway casualness of a juvenile lead, "Well, you have caught me out, haven't you? How clearly we both remember my dulcet words not half an hour ago: 'This is the first time I've been on this boat.' And lo, the evidence is in your fair hands. The very scarf I chose for my niece's birthday on the occasion of our first meeting. It's a fair cop, as the criminal classes are wont to say."

"What is it doing here?"

"What indeed?"

"There was no birthday, no niece?"

"Quite right. My brother has, as far as I know, no children."

"Then why? Why did you buy it? And then leave it here? Did you give it to Taylor to give away, perhaps?"

"How kind you are, Ginny. Even now looking for extenuating circumstances. How sorry I am to hurt you. How sweet you were to kiss. How sorry I am."

"But, Robert, why?"

He straightened up. The shy, lanky student whose untidy fair hair fell so endearingly over his forehead vanished for the last time. The man of the world took his place, but a sharper, more knowing, and more ruthless man of the world who used his charm for his own ends and played with trust and emotion and loyalty, treating them as weaknesses to be exploited.

Ginny watched the change come over him with an almost impersonal curiosity. So many lies, so many turns and twists. As he spoke, she grew sad, so sad she felt weighed down with it. She had felt no passion for him, nor did she believe she ever would have done. It was the betrayal of friendship that hurt, the loss of what might have been an affectionate and healing love, the knowledge that she had been used.

The sense of danger emerged much more slowly, faint signals that grew in strength with every word Robert said, with every shift of his expression.

"I bought the scarf in order to get to know you. That should be fairly obvious, surely. And a tedious business it was, waiting until you were the only assistant free to serve me. And those peripatetic lunch hours of yours. I had to go to the shop twice before I saw you there at all. Out at lunch, every time."

Ginny leaned against the hard edge of the sink. That felt real at least.

"Why go to all that trouble to make my acquaintance?" she asked him.

"How charming that sounds!" he declared. " 'Make my acquaintance.' And absolutely accurate, of course. That was exactly what I was doing. As for why, my dear Ginny, you know that. Because of the church, because of the objects Ben found in the church and gave to you."

The mention of Ben in connection with this new Robert shocked her, that and the realization that the implications were wider than a few lies about a niece.

"What objects?" she said. "What did Ben find? I don't know what you're talking about."

"Very good," he said. "Very touching, but it won't do, you know. It simply won't do."

She became aware that they were stopping. The engine note had changed. The boat had gradually slowed. Now the noise was cut off completely. She heard Taylor call something.

"You'd better come down here," Robert answered. He went farther up the saloon until he was blocking any move of Ginny's forward. Taylor entered from the companionway. He lounged against the entrance, looking from one to the other of them. They are both my enemies, Ginny thought, and I haven't the faintest idea why. It sounded ridiculous. But their faces weren't ridiculous.

"What's up?" Taylor said.

"I've been careless," Robert told him. "She's found a scarf that shouldn't be here. I bought it from her, you see. She wonders what it's doing here."

"It's an easy guess, isn't it?" Taylor said.

Ginny looked at Robert. "You've been living here, on the boat?"

"Got it in one. Give the lovely lady a coconut."

"All the time?"

"All the time I've had to be in this godforsaken town. Slept the sleep of the unjust in that very bunk there. And never told you a lie. You never asked me where I was staying."

"No, I didn't ask you." She shook her head. "I assumed—I don't know. A hotel."

I washed your breakfast plates, she was thinking. Two plates, two knives and forks, two mugs for tea.

"Ah! There's your mistake. Never assume, my dear Ginny. Assumptions are not only foolish but often dangerous. Isn't that right, Taylor?"

"But why did you come here at all?" Ginny asked. "And where does this boat fit in?"

"Now those are two clever questions. Aren't they clever questions, Taylor? Shall I tell her?"

"It doesn't matter now, does it?" Taylor said. "She'd have found all this out anyway soon enough."

"Well, Ginny," Robert said, "I had to come down here because one of our little group got nabbed. Unfortunate but not disastrous as it turned out. However, we temporarily lost our safe banking place, as you might put it. It had been threatened before, as I understand you know. This time we were pretty cautious. We may use it again, though that's not decided yet. It's convenient, and old habits die hard. But in the meantime, we used the church. And that's where you came in. Because your son and heir found something of ours and gave it to you, and we want it back, Ginny dear, very quickly indeed."

Ginny felt as if she had been drawn into some nightmare game in which everyone but she knew the rules or engaged in a charade in which she had been the one to stand outside the door while the word was chosen and now stood within the circle of laughing faces, trying desperately to guess from such meager clues what all the company already knew.

"And the boat," he was continuing, "that's pretty obvious, I should have thought. Good engines, innocent fishing trips, only every fourth or fifth a little bit different. A rendezvous in the Channel, ten minutes at most, then back again. Safe as houses. You've had no more than two

spot checks from the customs boys in over two years—
have you, Taylor?—and each time on the way home.
They worry about what you're bringing in these days,
drugs, illegal immigrants and so on, more than about
what you're taking out. We wouldn't touch cargoes like
that. Everything small and manageable and very, very
valuable, that's the firm's policy. And to answer your next
question before you ask it, why have we brought you out
here? If you cast a look through the nearest porthole,
you'll see, well, not very much: a reedy bank, a bit of
mud. Taylor discovered this spot. A miniature ravine, you
might say. Instead of a boat sticking up on the skyline,
like anywhere else on the marsh, you can't see it until you
trip over it, even at high water. It's a good meeting place.
Secret and isolated. And that's what we've all come for,
you as well. A meeting. So now you know."

Ginny put her hands to her face, forcing herself to
think carefully. Out of the confusion two points at least
were perfectly clear. They thought she had possession of
something of theirs, something stolen, and second, they
thought that Ben had found it and given it to her.

"Where is Ben?" she said. She turned from one to the
other. "Where is he? What have you done to him? You
didn't see him running along the riverbank, did you, Taylor? You haven't seen him at all. Or have you taken him
away? Have you hurt him? Where is he?"

The men listened to her quite unmoved. Robert was
even smiling a little. "He's all right. He had a tumble
down the steps in the church, as you thought, but he
didn't damage himself. Taylor had just made sure he was
all right when you came bursting into the saloon. He's in
there, in the forward cabin, sleeping."

"Let me see him. Ben? Ben!"

Robert stopped her rush forward. He barred her way
with ease and, when she tried to push past him, held her
arms. She was breathless, with relief and anger mingling
with apprehension and fright. For a moment she re-

mained quite still in Robert's imprisoning embrace, such a different embrace from their last. He looked down at her and said softly, "Am I still the chameleon? Or the leopard?"

"Let me go, Robert," she said in a low, even voice. "If you've harmed him, I'll kill you."

He laughed. "The tigress and her cub. Who'd have thought gentle Ginny to be so fierce a cat? All right. I've no objection. It merely proves the idea was right."

"What idea?"

"Simply, that if we hold Ben, you'll tell us straight away what you've done with the diamonds. Your child is worth more to you than diamonds, isn't he?"

She struggled against his grip, calling as loud as she could, "Ben!"

"We haven't harmed him," Robert protested. "We haven't touched him. For God's sake, Taylor, throw me the key."

Taylor tossed the key the length of the saloon. Robert caught it and unlocked the bulkhead door.

The forward cabin was small and cramped, with less headroom than the saloon. It had two narrow berths, one on either side, following the curve of the bow, and was being used mainly as a stowage compartment.

It was empty.

8

WHEN THEY CARRIED him down from the church and put him on a berth in the forecabin with a blanket thrown over him and an injunction to rest from his fall and he'd soon feel better and why he'd thought they'd wanted to hurt him heaven only knew, Ben had fallen asleep from a combination of emotional and physical exhaustion.

He slept as only a frightened eight-year-old can, whose games of chase and attack have suddenly become reality, whose friends have turned into confusing figures of unknown motives and reliability, and who wishes deep down below the surface of his conscious mind that it was nighttime and he was safe in bed with a full stomach from a good supper and his mother at hand to kiss and cuddle him if he should be troubled by bad dreams.

The revving of the boat's engines woke him. He lay at first wondering, then remembering, where he was. And he knew, as if it were a problem that had been hammered out and resolved while he slept, that somehow he had to get away from this cabin and this boat and find his mother and tell her everything that had happened. She would know what to do. It was no good lying there and trying to pretend that there was nothing odd about the way Mr. Travis had behaved. They had chased him, and they had wanted to hurt him, and they would too, if he didn't look out.

He sat up and examined himself in a methodical way. His trousers were torn and a pocket split by his fall in the church. One leg grazed by the stairs was stiff and sore, and he felt bruised all over. He had lost most of the things out of his pocket; but his penknife, which he carried in a back pocket, was also tied by a piece of string to his belt for safe keeping, and that was still there. He counted that as his first piece of luck, though to be honest he had to admit it was only due to his own foresight he still had that.

Next he had a good look at the cabin. He could tell he was in the bow of the boat by the way the sides of the cabin came to an angle. The door was locked, which, though it confirmed his suspicions and should have been no surprise, was still capable of making his mouth go dry and his heart beat as if he had been running. There was no point in trying to open the door with his penknife because he would have to go through the saloon and past the helmsman. He looked in the cupboards under the bunks, but they were full of things like tarpaulins and sou'westers and boots with nothing particularly helpful or nothing that he could think how to use.

He thought they were moving quite fast now. The engines made a throbbing noise, and it felt fast. He couldn't tell because there were no portholes in the cabin. What there was was a trapdoor in the roof, like the one that used to lead to the loft in their old house, and when he saw that, Ben felt a sudden leap of excitement because trapdoors opened. It wasn't called a trapdoor on boats, he remembered, it was called a hatch, but it was the same idea. You pushed upward, and it opened.

If he closed his eyes and concentrated very hard, he

could draw a picture of the boat in his mind as it had looked the first time he had seen it down on the marshes, and in that picture the deck where the hatch would open was hidden from the helmsman by the roof of the main saloon. So if he could get out, he had a chance of getting away unseen.

He climbed on top of the bunk and stretched his hand up to the hatch. He could reach it all right, but he couldn't get any kind of thrust on it. He got down and tugged the mattress off the second berth and piled it on top of the first and put the two deep cushions on top of that. It was an uneasy kind of tower to stand on, soft and seeming about to collapse when he moved his feet, but it did bring him near enough to the hatch cover to give it a hefty shove. Nothing happened. He pushed again and again until his hands felt as bruised and aching as the rest of him, and still the cover would not give an inch. He slid down to the floor and sat on the edge of the bunk for a rest and a think.

They were still moving, and he couldn't expect to escape until the boat was moored unless he was prepared to swim for it, and he hadn't much faith in the four strokes of breaststroke which were all he usually managed to achieve before sinking like a stone. But he ought to be ready to run for it as soon as they stopped.

Suppose they were going out to sea! How would he ever get away then? That terrible thought got him back up on the bunk for another go at the hatch. It still wouldn't move, and he was beginning to despair when suddenly he noticed what haste and anxiety had led him to miss before: the two bolts, one on either side, which were holding the hatch cover secure. The first bolt was fairly easy to shift, but the second was beyond his reach. He obtained a meager purchase on the edge of the hatch and, balancing precariously on the rim of the bunk, swung out until the fingers of his free hand just grasped the tip of the bolt. It took three attempts before he got enough leverage to pull it back, and when it loosened, he lost his balance and fell heavily on the floor between the bunks. He caught his elbow as he fell, and for minutes he lay on the bare planks, holding his arm and trying not to cry. It was the sound of the key being inserted in the lock which frightened him into action. He leaped onto the bunk where he had been left, flinging the two cushions wildly onto the opposite berth, pulled the blanket over him, and shut his eyes. He heard the door open and wondered what they would think when they saw he had moved the mattress from the second bunk, but no sooner was the door open than it was shut again, the lock clicking to.

It was warning enough. They might come back anytime, and if they noticed the hatch bolts unfastened, his chance of escape would be over. Better to risk the river than stay cooped up in the cabin. Fired by a now-reckless determination, he once more built up his pile of cushions, climbed on top, and pushed fiercely against the hatch. This time it gave. He stood on his toes, got a grip on the outside of the hatch with both hands, and shoved first with his head and then, as the cover began to swing open on its hinge, with his shoulders, hauling himself through the gap to land on his belly on the deck. He replaced the hatch cover and hid himself, crouching under the shelter of the main cabin roof. Only then did he dare raise his head and look around.

They were moving slowly down a deep and narrowing channel which appeared to be growing deeper every moment. Ben lay still and watched as the banks rose level with the deck. Something was different about the boat. The engines didn't seem as loud. Perhaps that was because he was farther away from them. Then he realized with consternation that they were stopping. The engines cut out altogether, and a moment later, he shrank back as he caught a glimpse of Taylor on the towpath, making the boat fast. It could only mean one thing. They had found him gone, and in another second they would be searching the boat. As soon as Taylor disappeared, he dashed across the deck and took a running jump at the farther bank. He slipped and began to roll, clutching at the fragile stalks of grasses to save himself. Somehow he scrambled up the last foot onto level ground and began to run.

He ran at first blindly, without any sense of direction, trying only to get some distance between himself and his pursuers, expecting any second to hear their shouts behind him. But he got a stitch in his side and had to stop and bend over to get his breath, and with the pause came the sense enough to prompt him to take cover. He lay flat on the ground, panting and trying to get his bearings. They had come miles, it seemed to him. No house, no roads were visible, only the creek, the wasteland and what must be, way over there, the embankment of the river. If he could reach the embankment, he could follow it all the way home. But they would know that too, and if he went back that way, they would be waiting for him.

His mother had given him instructions once on what to do if he was lost or in danger: (a) stop a policeman, (b) if no policeman, go into a shop and ask the shopkeeper for help, (c) go into a telephone box and ask for their home number, reversing the charges; if no reply, ask the operator to ring the police, and (d) as a last resort, he was allowed to stop a lady in the street, and if she had children with her, so much the better, as his mother said she would be more likely to help.

Ginny had been worried in case she confused him with all these alternatives, but she would have been pleased to know how methodically Ben now considered the best way to follow her advice. Since there were no policemen, and no shops in sight, and no telephones and no ladies, with or without children, he decided he would look for a road and then go along it until he did come to either (a), (b), or (c). He didn't think that (d) would be much use in his present circumstances. When he set off again, he therefore struck inland, away from the river.

Now all the long hours of stalking through Mrs. Sendall's garden, all the careful forays of reconnaissance, came to his aid. He moved at a steady pace, sometimes bent low, sometimes on all fours. Looking back, he twice saw the figure of a man, but he was a long way away and seemed to be searching toward the river. Ben was making for a line of poplars, which would for a while provide him with better cover, and, when he approached them, was pleased to find that they were lining a road. As he came through the trees and onto the road, he saw there was a car parked there. It was empty. He wondered whether to stay by it in case the owner returned or to walk on. He decided to walk. As he turned away, a man came from the shelter of the trees and spoke his name. It was James Aldous.

"I've been waiting for you, Ben," he said. "I saw you leave the boat. I was hoping you might come this way. You hide yourself very well. I lost you several times."

Ben said nothing. He no longer trusted his friends.

"You won't catch him. He'll be halfway home by now."

Ginny leaned against the door of the saloon and tried to radiate as much casual confidence as she could. Underneath she was sick with terror for Ben. How long he had been gone, where he had gone, if he was safe or injured or even dead were questions she couldn't dare allow herself to consider if she was to remain calm and in control.

Robert was lounging on the seat, a bottle of whiskey and a glass on the table in front of him. They had been alone in the locked saloon for ten minutes, ever since Taylor had gone to search for Ben.

"Taylor will find him," Robert drawled. "He'll be

somewhere along the embankment. He won't have got far." He poured another finger of spirit into the glass. "Why don't you have some of this? I'm sure you need it."

"As much as you do?"

He smiled. "Claws still out, Ginny? There's no need, you know. There was never any harm intended to you."

"I don't think I quite believe that, Robert, not now."

"What I can't understand," he remarked thoughtfully, frowning over his glass, "is this holier than thou attitude. You've been behaving just as criminally as us, and you might as well admit it. Stealing by finding, it's called, I believe."

Ginny had given up trying to convince them she had never seen and certainly never taken any diamonds, either from Ben or anyone else. She almost wished she had. At least she would have had some weapon to bargain with. Perhaps she should pretend she had got them, but she would have to be careful or she would be maneuvered into having to produce them—or be locked in here while one of the men went to fetch the stones from their mythical hiding place, and her position after that would be far worse than it was now.

She became aware of how tired she was, and how hungry. She hadn't eaten since her early breakfast, and that seemed a very long time ago.

"It's terribly hot in here," she said. "Can't we have the door open?"

"And risk you leaping for your life? No, thank you. I'd catch you, and no one would see or hear you; but it's too tiring to contemplate. One Benson loose is quite enough." He paused. "You know, Ginny, you ought really to be cheering Taylor on, hoping he finds your lost lamb. It would be better than drowning, better than being trapped in the mud flats when the tide goes out. You can die of exposure, you know, even in summer."

"It's no good trying to frighten me," Ginny said. "I know Ben. He'll be all right."

"I'll admit he's turned out to be far more enterprising than I would have anticipated. I thought his fall in the church would have kept him quiet far longer. But even if he did get home, Ginny, what would he find? You missing, Mrs. Sendall in hospital. Right, he's a bright child, and he manages to find his way to the police. You're not going to tell me there won't be many hours' delay before anyone does anything about a small boy's story of kidnapping. They'll think it's fantasy, storytelling."

"I think they'll take him seriously," Ginny said. "After what happened to Mrs. Sendall."

"Ah, now you see that's the sort of remark that leads to trouble. A more devious character would have nodded and said, 'Quite right, Robert, quite right,' and attempted to lull me into thinking both of you completely harmless. I understand why you act in this foolish way because I understand you. You are one of those unfortunate people who cannot help telling the truth and when in trouble cannot stop themselves attempting to fight back."

"I could be devious if I wanted, Robert," she said mildly, "but I despise you too much to bother."

He didn't reply. He looked at her in silence with a thoughtful, cold expression that reminded her of the way Taylor had looked at her. She had not been frightened of Robert before, but that look frightened her. It made her realize as she had never done before, because she had never come in contact with it before, a fact elementary in its simplicity: that the people who commit crimes are different from those who do not in that there is something missing in them. The capacity for concern has eroded away. The selfishness necessary for an act of crime was like a cancer, which, beginning as no more than a pinhead, grows with voracious appetite, eating up the normal cells of the character, until the gratification of the monstrously swollen ego is the sole purpose left in life. The original personality becomes unbalanced, mutilated, and finally destroyed. And of that disease, indifference was a symptom.

She was to recognize that cold and dangerous conceit in yet another person before the end of that day. Robert spoke of him, and his first words were a warning.

"You want to curb your tongue when the third member of our team arrives," he remarked. "He's a little more ruthless than me. He wouldn't like to hear you talk so disparagingly about his colleagues. Let me advise you to tread carefully with him. He can be pretty vicious at times."

"So there is another one of you," Ginny said. "Is that who you've come out here to meet?"

"That's right." He glanced at his watch. "He should be here any minute now. He won't be pleased if we've lost the boy. He suggested taking him. He knows how fond you are of Ben. Listen, and you might hear his car. You know that car, of course, you've been in it. Don't pretend his identity will be a surprise to you. You've known who he is for some time. You might as well admit it. You see, he has told me about your various interesting conversations. It may surprise you to know he still admires you. As a woman, that is. He doesn't think very much of your common sense. Of course, he doesn't understand you as I do."

Ginny sat down on the berth opposite Robert. She felt in some extraordinary way as if she had been stabbed to the heart. She had not expected there to be a third man, or rather she had hoped when Robert had betrayed himself that he and Taylor were in it alone.

She was a fool, as Robert had said. To trust both, to be deceived by both. But why should it be such a bitter shock to have her suspicions confirmed? Far, far worse than learning about Robert, about whom she had had no doubts? Shouldn't she feel pleased with herself that she had seen through James from the beginning? "He can be pretty vicious." A good description of Mrs. Sendall's attacker.

"Was he the one who tried to gas me?" she asked.

"I'm afraid so. That was done purely on impulse, he told me, if that is any consolation to you. He hadn't planned to kill you; but you went back to the house unexpectedly, and it seemed opportune."

And afterward, she remembered, he had joked and been kind and had looked after Ben.

"Was that why you took Ben and Mrs. Sendall out that day for a picnic on the river?" she asked Robert. "To leave the house empty?"

"If we had found the diamonds," he pointed out in the most reasonable way, "none of this unpleasantness would have been necessary. We searched that house from end to end. Where have you put them, Ginny? Not in your bank, surely?"

"And when you came back from London, when I was worried and wanted to get back to the house, you kept me out, insisted on dinner, made us delay and delay, so he could search the house again, and because of that, Mrs. Sendall could die."

"That was my part at that stage, to keep you away. I do what I'm told, Ginny, like any good lieutenant."

"That's not a very savory excuse, is it, after all that's happened in the world?"

Robert sighed. "You won't get anywhere trying to start discussions on ethical behavior. I have no ethics, except those of get what you can, when you can. Like everybody else. Even you, Ginny, even you."

"All right. So you feel no responsibility. Except, I suppose, to him. Is he the boss?"

He nodded. "He's the older. It was his idea, his organization, and he takes most of the profit." He turned and looked through the porthole beside him. "And here he comes. I'd know the note of that car's engine anywhere. I think he must have picked Ben up, too. There's someone else in the car. Go and sit over there, while I unlock the door. Go on!"

Ginny obeyed. She was thinking that Ben would have run to James if he saw him. He would still think of him as his friend. She said as calmly as she could, "What does he intend to do with Ben and me? Another suicide attempt, successful this time? Or an accident on the river, with both drowned. Which way are you going to kill us, Robert?"

"I've killed no one, Ginny," Robert said. "What happens to you is not my concern. And remember, you've brought all this on yourself."

He unlocked the door and then sat down again. He watched Ginny. He was no longer smiling. When she met his eyes, he looked away. She could hear the car now. It stopped. There was a slamming of doors. She heard voices, indistinct, unidentifiable; the sound of footsteps on the deck, coming down the companion steps. The door opened. The figure of a man filled the doorway.

"Good afternoon, Mrs. Benson," said Morgan. "How very pleasant to meet you again."

"Well, I don't know how else to convince you," said James, "except by letting you do the phoning. But we can't hang about. We must let the police know where the boat is."

For the past five minutes, he had been endeavoring to win Ben's confidence, coaxing him as he would have coaxed a wild deer to feed from his hand, but Ben, like the deer, wouldn't come near him. He backed away, every time.

"The phone box is half a mile up the road," James said. "They're expecting a call from me, whether I've managed to find anything or not. I know you've had a rotten time, Ben, and you feel nervous about getting into the car. I appreciate that. You're acting very sensibly. Your mother would be proud of you. So how about you staying here and keeping watch with the binoculars while I go and phone?"

Ben didn't know what to do. He didn't want to be caught again. On the other hand, he didn't want to be left alone. But wouldn't it be safer to be left alone? Or would James just fetch the others.

"You do know your mother's on that boat, don't you?" James said.

Ben stared. "She's not. She can't be."

James nodded. "She must be. She told me Robert Travis was coming to collect both of you at one and take you to lunch. I went to talk to the police, and when I left them, I went back to your house. I hoped you'd both be back. I found the front door unlocked. Your mother's handbag was in the hall. I searched for you both. I went to the church. I found these."

From his trouser pocket he produced the piece of blue and white crockery, the heavy green bottle glass. He held his hand out, the palm upward, the two treasures resting on it. Ben gazed at them. His glance moved from them to James' face.

"I went to the creek," James continued. "The boat had gone. I fetched my car and drove out here. I wasn't sure exactly where the hiding place was, but I knew it must be within walking distance of that pub where the bus stops, where you and your mother had got off on the day of your picnic. That creek seemed the only one deep enough to take the cruiser. I've been watching with my binoculars. The boat was well hidden. I wasn't sure where it was until you came bounding over the bank. I thought your mother might be with you. I thought she might have helped you to escape."

"Nobody helped me," Ben said. "I opened the hatch by myself."

"I see."

"I didn't see my mother. Do you really think she's on the boat?"

"I think she is wherever Robert Travis is."

Ben thought it over.

"I'll come with you," he said.

"Thank you for your confidence," James said. He spoke seriously. He opened the car door. Ben climbed into the passenger seat. James went around the other side and got into the driver's seat. He turned to Ben. "All right?"

Ben nooded. "Can I have my things?"

James handed them over. Ben held them tight, one in each hand. They were two of his favorites. He felt that things were going to be all right now.

"How is the time, Taylor?" Morgan sat at the table, magisterial in presence, bland as ever in manner. It was now Robert who leaned against the door. Taylor had been told to sit next to Ginny. His search had been in vain. Morgan had picked him up as he drove up to the boat and told him to stop wasting his time.

"The boy is unimportant now. We have his mother. What is important is the rendezvous."

"It's getting late," Robert observed.

Taylor nodded. "We're cutting it fine. We mustn't miss the tide."

"I am well aware of the importance of the tides." Morgan turned to Ginny. "You see, my dear, we haven't very much time. You're not going to keep us waiting any longer, are you? You've already wasted a great deal of my time."

"It is once a month you take the stolen property you have collected out of the country, that's right, isn't it?" She had not got over her surprise at finding Morgan the head of this syndicate, and yet the more she thought about it, the more obvious it became. And it wasn't James. James had nothing to do with it. James was a friend. Even in this situation, she couldn't stop smiling at the marvelous relief of that discovery.

Morgan had raised an eyebrow in weary tolerance. "I am glad you find this so amusing, Mrs. Benson. I have canceled one rendezvous because of you. I don't intend to cancel this one."

"We'll have to go without the gems," Taylor said. "Unless you can get them from her in the next ten minutes."

"That's hardly likely, is it?" Morgan reproved him. "She won't be carrying them around in her handbag. I presume you have checked her handbag?"

Robert and Taylor exchanged glances. Their expressions made Ginny laugh. She was beginning to feel lightheaded anyway. Hunger and anxiety and fear, combined with the shock of Morgan's appearance and the delight of James' innocence, were inspiring in her a kind of reckless carelessness. She was in a mood to do and say anything.

"I haven't got my handbag with me," she remarked. "I don't usually carry it around with me in my own garden. I went out to look for Ben, to tell him to get ready for our lunch with Robert. I hadn't intended to come for a cruise. And that's bad luck for you, Robert, isn't it? If you hadn't kidnapped Ben, we could have all gone out to lunch together, you and me and Ben and my handbag."

There was a stricken silence. Then Morgan began to laugh. He rocked with his laughter. He slammed his fist down on the table in an ecstasy of amusement. "Robert, for a womanizer you know little of women. In her handbag! What safer place! Always with her, night and day. Never get-at-able. She had the diamonds with her all the time. While she dined with you, and Taylor and I had to silence that foolish old woman in order to search the house, the diamonds were on the dinner table in front of you. No doubt bathed in romantic candlelight."

"There were no candles," Ginny observed. "It was a very dreary meal."

"Dreary, she calls you, you hear, Robert. And you

were getting on so well, you told me. Had I ever known your charm to fail, you asked me. My poor boy!"

Robert was looking sullen. "I kept her away from the house."

"Not on one occasion, you didn't." Morgan extended his white hand to Ginny. "I'm very glad you recovered, my dear. It would really have made little difference if the suicide attempt had succeeded. I was forgetting there is no need for violence when there is a child concerned."

His affability was more chilling than the others' threats. "What do you mean?"

"I had intended to kill you, because you knew too much and you were dangerous. But once you have handed over the diamonds, I shall leave you in peace. You see, I know you won't go to the police. Not as long as there is a small boy about. You can't chain a boy to the house forever. He will go out sometime. To play, to go to school. You understand me, Mrs. Benson. One word, and it is the boy who has the sad but fatal accident."

She looked him in the eyes, and she nodded her head. She was quite sure he would kill Ben. She was quite sure that he intended to kill her, too, no matter what assurances she gave him. He had killed her husband because he had discovered what was going on. It was a death that must have been worth it to them because they had continued since then with no suspicion and no interruption. Why should they hesitate once again to make themselves safe?

"Are you going to fetch the diamonds now?" Taylor asked Morgan. "You want us to wait?"

"No." He shook his head. "We can't wait. We can't miss another rendezvous. Get ready. Mrs. Benson and I will leave when you're ready to go."

"Have you a large haul to take this time?" Ginny asked, with a pretense at calm interest.

"Not bad. Robert brought it back from London. He

had it in his pocket when you dined. It's amusing, isn't it?
All those precious stones in one small area, and neither of
you knowing what the other possessed."

"It wasn't so amusing for my husband," Ginny said.

Morgan said nothing. He jerked his head sharply at
Taylor and Robert, and they both went out. Ginny heard
them moving about, checking the engines she supposed,
making ready for the voyage.

Morgan got up. He took two clean glasses from the
cupboard by the galley and carefully poured a tot of
whiskey into each. He handed one to Ginny. She accepted
it. They sipped in silence.

"I didn't intend to kill him," Morgan said suddenly.
"An opportunity presented itself, that's all. I am an op-
portunist, Mrs. Benson. I have been all my life. I have not
had an easy life. I had disadvantages as a boy that it took
some doing to overcome. I won't bore you with the details. They had the effect at least of making me determined to become someone in this town, someone in the
world. Robert began it. He stole something, and because
he was a fool, he didn't know how to sell it or obtain its
value. He came to me. I found a place for it. He brought
me more. I sat down and considered the possibilities. I
analyzed the situation. I foresaw the weaknesses, the mis-
takes that lead to capture, and I devised a plan not to
eliminate them entirely as such things can never be elimi-
nated, but to reduce them to the lowest possible level. For
example, I told Robert to stay in London. The goods
were fetched by another man, who I set up in a secondhand bookshop. The bookshop you know about, of
course. When the cache was the right size, Taylor took
one of his fishing trips and handed the goods to our Am-
sterdam agent, shall I call him. The money was trans-
ferred to the bookshop account—another rare book sold.
Unfortunately your husband not only realized that no rare
books ever entered the shop, but did actually one day see
Charlie putting something away in the safe. He was puz-

zled. Charlie explained it away, but he warned me Mr. Benson might not be satisfied. We couldn't have the police looking into that bookshop, for no matter how slight a reason. I was worrying over the problem one day when I happened to see your husband's car awaiting collection at my garage. You did know I owned that garage, I presume? I went back that night, unlocked the garage, let myself in, and loosened the steering box housing. I wasn't sure what the result would be, or when. It was bit of luck that he undertook that long journey that very weekend. It might have happened anywhere. It happened a good long way away from my bookshop, I'm glad to say. Very sad for you, of course, my dear. No one suspected it was anything but an accident. I gather you yourself were of the opinion your husband had fallen asleep."

"How did you know that?" Ginny said.

"I made inquiries, naturally."

"Did you know he had made an appointment to talk to the police the following week?"

He shrugged. "If you are to survive in any business, Mrs. Benson, you need the kind of foresight I possess. You also have to be lucky. My luck has always been good. Yours, I fear, has not. You shouldn't have moved into the town. That was your mistake." He cocked his head and listened attentively. "We must be off in a moment. Another whiskey?"

"What difference did it make, my moving into the town?" Ginny asked.

"I had decided you knew nothing, that your husband had told you nothing. Your move, your coming to see me, changed my mind. I wondered why on earth you should give up a piece of sound property to come and stay with an old lady in a derelict house. I suppose your husband left a letter, a note which only came to light a long time after his death. I don't suppose you'll tell us now. A pity. I'm interested."

"I'm interested too," Ginny said. "In the way your mind worked."

He leaned back against the cushion in a genially expansive manner. A relaxed gentleman dealing kindly with a rather silly client. "I tried to do my best for you, Mrs. Benson. I endeavored to discover what you were after. Then the diamonds vanished. I told Robert to get to know you. We made sure the tramp who frequented the church hadn't found the stones and kept them or swopped them with another idiot for a pint of red biddy. Robert and Taylor watched the house and the church. Your son, madam, was the only other visitor to the church."

He used his voice very skillfully, Ginny noticed. He was playing it like an organ, rising to a diapason of dramatic sound with his last sentence. He dropped a tone or two in continuing his narrative. What he said bewildered Ginny.

"Then I learned, at the concert that you did indeed hold the diamonds."

"At the concert?" she said. "I don't understand."

"You told me yourself. You knew all about the bookshop, you said. 'The essential things' was the way you put it. You knew all about the property. We discussed my buying it back."

Morgan had come to them, Ginny remembered, and dismissed Robert with some story about his car being badly parked, so he could talk to her. And that was what it had been about.

"I thought you meant my house!" she said.

"And when I paid money into your bank, I suppose you thought that was for the house? It won't wash, you know. It was a good offer. I was prepared to let it be merely the first installment of a larger sum. Considering the diamonds are my property, I have been more than generous to you. You have been playing very hard to get, haven't you, my dear, and where did it lead to? The woman who befriended you will die."

"She's not dead," Ginny protested. "She'll recover."

"I can't allow her to recover," Morgan said. "She, also, has learned too much."

"Why?" Ginny cried. "What is it you want? To be the biggest frog in the pond?"

The engines suddenly started. They roared, then quieted as Taylor throttled them down. Robert came down the companion steps. They were ready to go. They were going to leave her alone with Morgan.

"Why?" she repeated desperately. "Because your mother married beneath her? Because she made you ashamed of having been born?"

His face was as white as a slab of lard. He hissed the words: "Where did you hear this? Who told you about me? Robert? Was it Robert?"

"I've told her nothing," Robert said. He shook his head at Ginny. "I warned you. I told you to keep quiet."

"I wanted to know," she said coldly. "I wanted to know why he considers himself more important than a woman like Mrs. Sendall and a child like Ben."

"Who are they?" Morgan said. "What are they to me? They've had everything given to them on a plate. Whoever helped me? Who, in this town? I've fought for my place, and I intend to hold it. Money's hard to get when you have nothing. Well, two years ago I discovered how to get my own capital, fast, with no worry about tax. There's one thing I've learned, Mrs. Benson. Money and land equal power in our society. That's what I'm after; that's what I'll get. Before very much longer, I'll own this town, and that's only the beginning. They respect me already. They'll do more than that before I'm through."

"They don't respect you," Ginny said. "They see through you. They tolerate you. They will always remember everything about you."

There was a long and rather frightening silence. Robert said at last, "We should go if we're going. We'll be stranded on the mud if we don't."

Morgan got to his feet.

"Come on," he said to Ginny. There was no more music in his voice, no more striving for effect. It was a bleak command. He gripped her arm and guided her up the steps. He didn't speak to Robert or Taylor. It was Robert who helped her onto the bank.

"If I were in a dramatic frame of mind," she said to him, "I would say to you 'Remember me.' "

"Ginny—"

"You do know what he's going to do, don't you, Robert? He's going to kill us both, me and Ben. He'd kill us even if I had the diamonds, which I have not. And he's then going to the hospital to stop Mrs. Sendall's mouth. Don't you see that he's mad? Don't you realize you must stop him?"

Robert wouldn't look her in the face. He turned away. She put a hand on his sleeve. "You'd be wiser to stay on the other side of the Channel. Take that little cache of gems you have in the boat and keep it." His head jerked around, and she smiled. "So that is what you plan to do, is it? Good luck, Robert."

They had put a tarpaulin over the car in which Morgan had arrived, and when he pulled it off, she understood why. The bright red of the MGB would stand out for miles.

"So poor Robert didn't even own this," she said.

"Poor Robert owns nothing," Morgan said. He opened the car door. "Get in."

Ginny obeyed. Morgan got in and started the car. They bumped unevenly along the grassy track to the road. As soon as they reached a level surface, he began to drive fast, too fast, Ginny realized, for her to jump out without killing herself.

"We'll go straight to your house and collect the diamonds," Morgan said. "Then we'll find your son. It is more than likely that he is waiting for you there."

And if he is, Ginny thought, that will be the end of

both of us. Ben darling, she willed him, run to the police;
wherever you are, don't go home.

As they turned from the single-lane side road onto a
wider B-road, Ginny heard an unmistakable noise overhead. She peered upward through the window, trying to
get a glimpse of it.

"What is it?" Morgan said.

"Nothing."

The helicopter clattered on toward the river. It will go
right over the boat, Ginny thought. If only the people on
board the helicopter knew what was going on, they could
stop all this. There was nothing she could do. Even if she
had wound down the window and waved and screamed,
they probably wouldn't have noticed, and if they had,
they would merely have thought she was waving to them
out of friendliness.

She had been expecting them to drive through the
hamlet where she and Ben had left the bus on the day of
their picnic, but she suddenly realized they were going in
the opposite direction.

Morgan glanced at her and smiled. "We are going the
long way around. A minor precaution but one worth taking. These small details are the sort of things that have
contributed to my success."

He was patronizing her again. His voice was smug and
self-satisfied. The brief wound she had inflicted on him
was quite healed over. He had convinced himself once
more of her unimportance.

She looked at his plump profile and hated him. She
thought of her husband, she thought of Ben deprived of
his father and made miserable and frightened by the activities of this man. She thought him stupid and cruel. She
wasn't going to let him kill her and Ben and Mrs. Sendall.
She wasn't going to allow it.

There was an avenue of trees ahead, poplars lining
both sides of the road. As they drew level with the first of
them, Ginny, acting almost without her own volition,

reached across and seized the wheel with both hands. The car veered across the road. Morgan fought her, pulling back. He was swearing and shouting at her. He took one hand off the wheel and tore at her hands. She could not move them even if she had wished. They seemed locked into position. Morgan stamped on the brake, and they went into a wild skid. In the last second he reached forward and switched off the engine, but it was too late.

James and Ben heard the crash from halfway across the fields. They had been signaling to the helicopter, but there had been no urgency in it. The boat was visible enough now from the land, let alone from the sky. Taylor must have panicked when the pilot began to play with him, weaving from side to side above him like a sheepdog guiding in his sheep. He put the engines on full power, trying to escape. In the river he might have managed at that speed, but he was still in the creek, and it was long past high tide. He ran aground at the mouth of the creek, and he and Robert were still struggling to shift the boat when the helicopter landed and the arrests, as the official report put it, were made. The revenue men arrived by car soon afterward and found the hiding place of the gemstones with no difficulty. The second car, rendezvousing with James, found him pulling Ginny out of the wrecked MGB.

The car had hit one of the poplars, on the driver's side. Ginny had escaped with little more than bruises. Morgan, they discovered later, had fractured his skull. Ginny clung to James as the ambulance took Morgan away.

"I didn't mean to hurt him. I only meant to stop the car. I was going to run for it. I was going to hide among the dikes. Oh, Ben, oh, darling Ben!"

They had kept Ben in the police car until they were sure Ginny was all right. At James' nod he had come running forward. He didn't know he was crying. Ginny kissed and hugged him over and over again until his

enormous and overwhelming relief and happiness sim-
mered down into a normal contentment in which embarrassment at being embraced by his mother in front of policemen began to play a major part.

James drove them home. Ben sat on the front seat of
the car between him and Ginny and told her all his adventures right from the beginning. She held his hand tight
and listened and said only the right things. Halfway
through, she put her arm around his shoulders and drew
him against her, and he, temporarily forgetting his new
status as permanent honorary member of the police force,
an award made to him on the field of battle by Detective
Sergeant Wood in person, snuggled up close against her
breast and fell asleep.

James carried him into the house and deposited him,
still sleeping, on his bed.

"I'll come back later," he said. "If I may."

"I haven't thanked you," Ginny said. "I haven't apolo-
gized to you."

"Later," he said.

Ben woke up after twenty minutes, pleased to be home
and anxious for his tea. The adventures were already
blurring in his mind. He had forgotten the fears. All that
remained was the memory of the excitements. He demolished eggs and baked beans and half a fruitcake and suddenly remembered Alice.

"She's in the church, Mum," he cried. "She's had her
kittens. Come and see."

Nothing would stop him. And Ginny, reasoning that if
the church did give Ben the creeps when he saw it again,
nothing would make him go in, decided a walk down
there would do no harm. Besides, she was worried about
Alice, too.

They found her where they had both left her, curled in
the pulpit with her kittens. She looked pleased to see
them. She miaowed a greeting, an unusual gesture for her

since she normally spoke to them only once a day when she came in for her breakfast. That was a polite "good morning" cry. This was an expression of grudging satisfaction that they were deigning to take notice of her at last, combined with a demand for food. She came trotting down the steps to drink the milk they had brought her with a vigor that sent a spray of cream over the floor. Ben picked up the kittens and let them crawl over his shirt. Ginny, looking around at the broken staircase, the hanging plaster, decided it might be as well to get the council to board the place up more securely.

"Ben," she said, hoping that what she was going to say would not upset him, "the men in the boat said you found some diamonds in this church."

"They said they were diamonds. I think they're pebbles. I showed them to Mrs. Sendall, and she never said they were diamonds."

"What did you do with them?"

"We hid them. I told you. We played hide-and-seek."

"Where did you hide them?"

"Mrs. Sendall said to put them where I found them, and then she'd see if she was as clever as I'd been at seeking them."

"And did she find them again?" Ginny asked.

"Not unless she came back in the night. And I don't think she did. She said she was going to look in the morning, in proper daylight. But she was gone this morning. I think she must have forgotten them. They weren't meant to be left here. Only for the game. I came back to get them; only Mr. Travis and the other man chased me."

"Shall we see if they're still here?" Ginny said. She was wondering where on earth in the shambles, Morgan and Robert had found anything resembling a safe hiding place.

Ben didn't go far. He stood on the second of the pulpit steps, so that he was level with the wooden head of the banister post. The head was large and round with a thicker band of wood around the center. Ben put both hands on the top and pulled. It came apart like an Easter egg. Inside the hollow of the ball the eight uncut diamonds, as large and as opaque as small glass pebbles, lay snug and safe.

"Very special ones, the police say. They know where they come from and a value has been put on them of fifty thousand to seventy-five thousand pounds. Even allowing for cuts, that's not a bad capital sum to add to your bank balance, especially when you total it up with the rest of the stuff they estimate he's moved." Tom, in his professional capacity as reporter, was sitting on the sofa in the living room, with Eileen holding his hand. Eileen was there, she had announced, as baby-sitter.

"Mr. Aldous asked if you'd go to the hospital. Mrs. Sendall's come around. She's going to be all right, they say. Isn't it a relief?"

The police had been and taken away the diamonds. Ben had been told they were important evidence and had been stepped up to honorary sergeant in the force. He took his promotion with appropriate modesty.

"If he goes on like this," Sergeant Wood had told Ginny, "we'll all be able to retire with redundancy pay. By the way, the insurance company was offering a reward for the diamonds' recovery. We're putting your name forward."

Ben was in bed, whether asleep or not Ginny didn't mind. She thought he probably wasn't since he had demanded that Alice and the kittens spend the night in a basket in his room. She made Tom and Eileen sandwiches and coffee before she left. They talked, naturally enough, of nothing else but Morgan.

"His normal business was profitable enough," Tom said, "but he had to pay tax on that. This suited him far better."

"Were the police on to him at all?" Ginny asked.

"They'd heard of his existence through the grapevine. They knew there was a new fence who specialized only in the very, very top-grade stuff, but they hadn't tracked him down to this area. The first connection with the town came with the arrest of Charles Mayhew. Mayhew was born here, did you know that? Under a different name, I may say. He's a contemporary of Morgan's. They went to the same school."

"Well, well," Eileen said. "The old boy network. Would you believe it?"

"They didn't think much about it until Mr. Aldous asked one of his police friends in London if they'd ever heard of a Charles Mayhew. They knew that as one of Charlie's aliases, and when they heard he'd been running a secondhand bookshop, they got very interested. It's a fascinating story, isn't it?"

Eileen hugged him. "And you'll write it so beautifully, darling. You'll make your name with it. The press will be flocking down here. Ginny, start practicing your smile. Can't you see the caption? 'Mother and son trap diamond gang.' "

Ginny smiled. "I must go. Are you staying, Tom?"

"I'm driving you to the hospital."

"Thank you. I didn't realize—"

"Mr. Aldous gave me very strict instructions."

"Oh. I see."

"Give my love to the old girl," said Eileen.

As they drove to the hospital, Tom remarked with an engaging enthusiasm, "It's been marvelous meeting Mr. Aldous. I admire him enormously."

Ginny was at a loss how to take this. "Do you?" she said.

"Of course, I didn't realize at first it was him. I didn't know he used a pen name. But when I met him, I recognized him at once from his photographs. He's a true craftsman. It's a pleasure to meet a real professional who just gets on with it. Never drops below his own standards. Don't you think so? Or don't you read him?"

"I don't know what he writes," Ginny said truthfully.

"You must. James Firth. He writes thrillers. Very successful. There have been films of two of them."

She had seen them in libraries and bookshops. She had seen both the films. She didn't remember ever seeing his photograph.

"Oh, yes," she said weakly. "I know that name."

"Fancy him coming from around here. I didn't know Mrs. Sendall was his aunt."

"I don't think she is his actual aunt," Ginny said. "I think he's more of a friend of the family."

"Oh I see." He pulled up outside the hospital. "Anyway, lucky for you he was here. I gather he helped the police a lot."

The nurse who showed Ginny into Mrs. Sendall's room warned her not to stay too long.

"She did ask for you. But we want her to rest. If you'd just nip in and say hello so she can see you're all right."

Ginny nipped in. Mrs. Sendall was resting against the pillows in the shaded room. She was a tiny and slightly rakish figure in the tall hospital bed with her head bandaged like an eighteenth-century pirate. She looked tired but her old self again. She smiled delightedly at Ginny and lifted a delicate hand.

"Dearest Ginny, how glad I am to see you safe!"

Ginny kissed her cheek. "What a fright you gave us. Are you really better?"

"Oh, tush, it was nothing. It takes more than a bump on the head to put me under. I got the wrong man, though. I thought it was Robert, you know. Oh, I know he was involved, but I thought he was the one in the house that night looking for Ben's pebbles. It was because of the cigarette Ben found in the church. I knew it wasn't James, and Robert was the only other person who smoked those cigarettes. And the moment I met him, I thought I'd seen him before. It was only much later I realized why. He was the man I saw watching the house. I never saw his face clearly, but there was something so familiar about the way he stood and walked, the way he lighted his cigarettes."

"You shouldn't have tried to tackle him yourself. You should have stayed in your room."

"He would have searched there and no doubt hit me on the head anyway. I was worried about Ben. The sleeping pill didn't harm him?"

"I don't know how to thank you for the way you looked after him."

Mrs. Sendall smiled gently. "We all did very well, I think, Ginny, for two feeble women and a boy. You found the diamonds, I hear."

"That was clever of you, too."

"It's an old trick. Hide things in the most obvious place. I thought those thugs would never think of looking in their own hiding place. I would have gone into the church with Ben and seen where he put them, but I had to convince him it was a game."

"He stayed convinced. He still thinks it was a game. He's very resilient, I'm glad to say."

Mrs. Sendall patted the bed. "Sit down, dear. I've got a confession to make. You know James isn't my real nephew?"

"Yes, I did find out."

"I was sorry not to tell you. He asked me not to. He said he'll tell you himself. He's somewhere in the hospital. You will wait for him, won't you? He so wants to see you." She took Ginny's hand. "He's in love with you, Ginny. I expect you know that."

"Well—"

"Of course you do. And you love him whether you're aware of it or not. I can tell. No, don't protest. I'm very good at seeing these things. You loved your husband, and you mourned him, and now it's time to live again, Ginny.

Don't cry, dear, I know you've been under a terrible strain." She gripped Ginny's hand tighter. "Well, cry a little bit, if you want to. I feel like a weep myself. What a time you've had, haven't you, my dear? What a time you've had."

When Ginny left Mrs. Sendall, she found James standing in the corridor outside her room.

"Fraud," Ginny said to him.

"Ah! I see you've found me out."

"Wealthy thriller writer! What did you come down for? Copy?"

"You're not really cross, are you, Ginny?"

"How can I be cross with you? You've been saving all our lives."

He put his arms around her and kissed her hard.

"I love you," he said firmly.

"Maybe," she said. "Maybe. How can I believe a word you say? What did you come down for?"

He sighed. There was a bench against the wall. "Sit down," he said. "If you're determined to have the story of my life."

They sat down. James kept a firm hold of Ginny's hand.

"Mrs. Sendall's husband and my father were friends," he began, "and the families have kept in touch. When Mrs. Sendall noticed the house was once more being watched by strange men, she decided not to go to the police, who she knew could do little at that stage, but to ask my father for his advice. And my dad, who thinks writers are layabouts with nothing to do with their time, asked me to look into it. I rang Mrs. Sendall, and she asked me to come down for a few days. It was her idea to call me her nephew. She said her real nephew was in Canada and hadn't been back for years, so no one would know I wasn't he. And no one down here, she was certain, would ever associate me with the writer James Firth. The general idea was to find out what, if anything, was going on. So I started investigating everyone who came to the house or had anything to do with it, beginning naturally enough with Morgan. We thought it was a campaign to get Mrs. Sendall to leave the house. Of course, what it was was an attempt to get into the house and find those damned diamonds Ben had lifted so innocently."

"You suspected me, didn't you?" Ginny said. "Come on, admit it."

"Well, Morgan did seem to be getting after you a lot. All those intimate conversations, in his office, at the concert, and so on. Fred Stone said he liked beautiful women, so I thought perhaps it was plain lust. But it seemed a bit more than that."

"He thought Ben had given me the diamonds and I was doing a bit of hard bargaining over them."

"So I've gathered. Well, all my probing of Morgan led me to his marina project. But the bookshop business was still suspicious, and then the police identified Mayhew for me as a known thief, and Morgan was back in the center of things. It all began to make a picture. Morgan, Taylor, Mayhew; the thief, the bookshop, the boat, the fishing trips; the owner of the boat and the bookshop, who two years ago had suddenly acquired enough capital to buy up Dent's, for which he had previously been an able but not exactly wealthy employee. And in two years, he had built up the business to such an extent that he was not only the biggest agent and property dealer in the area but actually had sufficient funds at his command to plan something as ambitious as his marina complex. However, all that hadn't yet explained the connection with Mrs. Sendall's house. Why the intruders, growing ever more desperate and more dangerous? What was in the house that they wanted so badly? I thought the danger involved you, Ginny, and had finished with the gassing attack. I didn't think they'd attack Mrs. Sendall or I'd never have left, even for a night. Then we got the last link, and everything, as they say, fell into place."

"What last link?" Ginny said.

"Didn't I tell you? I took your advice about Somerset House. I got a friend to go there and search for the birth certificates of Robert Travis and Jack Morgan; I had given him the local police station number to ring if there was no answer from this number. The call came while I was at the police station. What he had found had interested him enough to search out the marriage certificates of their mothers. The same mother as it happened. Robert Travis and Morgan are half brothers."

Ginny stared at him. "The second marriage Mr. Stone mentioned."

"That's right. And both sons turned out as crooked as corkscrews. It can't have been the humble father Morgan so despised who had the bad blood. It must have been the respectable schoolmarm who felt she had married beneath her who had criminal tendencies."

"It explains a lot of things about Robert," Ginny said. "And the way Morgan treated him."

"It explained a lot of things to me about the way Robert Travis had been behaving toward you and Ben. I got back to the house fast. When I found you gone, Ben's things in the church, the boat gone, Taylor gone, I told the police. They decided it was worth a customs search, if I could trace the boat. I borrowed a car, and off I went. Fortunately they didn't waste much time after Ben and I had phoned. The helicopter spotted the red car, as well as the boat, but before the police could do anything about that, you'd done something about it yourself. I have never been so frightened as when I saw that car smashed against the tree. I thought you were dead."

"I thought I'd killed Morgan," Ginny said. "I don't ever want to think I've killed anyone again, even someone like him." She paused. "Sometimes you seemed so cold toward me. Did you really suspect me, James?"

"I had to. I was too much at the mercy of my feelings for you. I had to be cold-blooded and treat you as if you were capable of trickery and treachery and all the rest of it. If you had been and I'd allowed myself to be blinded by your beauty, Mrs. Sendall would have been the one to suffer."

"As a matter of interest," Ginny asked, "do you write your books in that effusive style?"

"My God," he said. "Every declaration of love sneered upon. How long are you going to hold out against my passion?"

"Oh, James—"

"I know, I know!" He stopped joking. "I'm sorry. I know what your husband meant to you. At least you know now you weren't responsible for his death. Do you think you can start living again now? I am serious, Ginny. I do love you. I love Ben, too. I think he's a very bright, brave child. Just like his mother. Are you going to force me to run away to television or wherever it is rejected lovers go now the foreign legion is out of fashion? I'm prepared to wait for you, you know. I'll wait a good long time. At least twenty-four hours. I'm afraid that's my limit. I'm not a Dobbin, you see. But I don't think you're an Amelia. And anyway I wouldn't talk like this if you hadn't clung to me the way you did after the crash."

"I don't have to marry you within twenty-four hours, do I?" Ginny asked.

"You don't have to marry me at all if you don't want to. I've no objection to living in sin."

"I think if you kissed me again," Ginny said, "it might help me make up my mind."

It was James who finally broke away. He got up, pulled her to her feet, and began to walk her along the corridor.

"What are you doing?" Ginny said.

"If it's persuasion like this you want," he said, "I am more than happy to provide it, but I feel I could do better in a more private place. We are going home."

Two days later Ginny and James brought Ben to see Mrs. Sendall. Overwhelmed with shyness at first at seeing her in such an unaccustomed place, and still not entirely sure what she was doing there, though her unfortunate tumble downstairs at her friend's house had been explained to him, Ben sat by the bed as quiet as a mouse, eating the box of candied fruit he had been given to bring as his present.

The adults talked not about what Morgan had done, but about what might happen to his schemes now.

"Are they still going to sell the allotments?" Mrs. Sendall wondered.

"I suppose so, in the end. They are not exactly rushing it. I think someone might suggest to them that they adapt the marina idea. I'm sure it's feasible and profitable even on a much smaller scale than Morgan's. You'll have to get Tom to put his paper on to it."

"Can you imagine what happened this morning?" Ginny said. "Dent's rang up. They've had an offer for my house."

"Good heavens above," Mrs. Sendall exclaimed. "I'd forgotten all about your house. What did you say?"

"I accepted like a shot. It's practically what we were asking for it, and I don't want to wait. I'm very glad it's being sold. It's for a family. Two boys they said. It's a good house for a family."

"Well. . . ." Mrs. Sendall smiled gently at her. "I'm very glad."

"And talking of property," James said, "how about selling half your house?"

"What an extraordinary idea! Who on earth to? And what would they do with half a house?"

"Well, we did think," said James, slipping his arm around Ginny's waist, "we could turn it into a family house, for me and Ginny and Ben."

Mrs. Sendall looked momentarily stunned. "Well, I'm all for it," she said at last. "I'd never have thought of it.

But you don't want to share a house with me, surely, even if you do have your own front door. You'll want to be off on your own."

"Off where?"

"I don't know. London. Wherever you're living now, James."

"I've been living in a small London flat and spending a lot of my time traveling. I can live anywhere. I only need my typewriter and paper and a lot of black coffee. I like it here and so does Ginny and so does Ben, and Ben's starting at school here." He paused. "We do intend getting married. I don't know if I made that clear."

She held out her arms. "Oh, Ginny. Oh, I am so pleased. Oh, Ben darling, are you pleased, too?" Ben smiled at James. He liked James.

"We brought champagne," Ginny said. "Will it make your head bad?"

"I don't give a damn if it does," said Mrs. Sendall. "And what is more, Ben shall have some too."

Ben cheered up now that interesting things were happening. He had his sip of champagne and, much encouraged, told Mrs. Sendall first about Alice and the kittens and then about his escape from the boat. She was a most satisfactory audience. She made *oohs* and *ahs* but never interrupted. When he had finished talking about himself, he felt it only polite to talk about her for a change.

"Mrs. Sendall," he said, "what did your husband do?"

She put her soft little hand on his and looked at him lovingly. "Would you like to know what he really did, Ben, with no jokes?"

"Yes," he said, surprising himself. "Yes, I would."

"It's not very exciting."

He said staunchly, "I shan't mind."

"Well, he was a tea merchant. He went up to London every day and went to an office and bought and sold tea."

"You mean in packets, like the grocer?"

"No, Ben, not in packets, in big chests. They have auctions, which means that a great many merchants go and bid for the tea when it comes into the country and they have to choose what they think will be the best tea at the best price."

"Does the tea come from China and India?"

"India and Ceylon and other places in the East. I'll show you in the atlas when I get home."

"I've seen pictures of tea merchants," Ben said excitedly. "I've seen them in my encyclopedia of different lives in different lands. They wear long gowns and have long mustaches. Did your husband have long mustaches?"

Mrs. Sendall exchanged a glance with Ginny, resigned, amused, apologetic.

"Yes, Ben," she said. "He had long mustaches and a gown of red damask and gold earrings in his ears, and he always spat out the tea when he tasted it."

Ben gave a huge, enthralled sigh. "Good Lord, Mrs. Sendall," he said, "that's the most interesting thing I've ever heard."

FAWCETT CREST
BESTSELLERS

THE CURSE OF THE KINGS *Victoria Holt*	Q2215	$1.50
THE DEVIL ON LAMMAS NIGHT *Susan Howatch*	P2213	$1.25
THE HOLLOW HILLS *Mary Stewart*	X2089	$1.75
THE DEVIL OF ASKE *Pamela Hill*	Q2094	$1.50
HARVEST HOME *Thomas Tryon*	X2082	$1.75
THE SEARCH FOR ANNA FISHER *Florence Fisher*	P2083	$1.25
MY LIFE IN THE MAFIA		
Vincent Teresa & Thomas C. Renner	X2072	$1.75
THE JESUIT *John Gallahue*	Q2073	$1.50
THE FINAL HOUR *Taylor Caldwell*	X2074	$1.75
LAUGHING ALL THE WAY *Barbara Howar*	Q2061	$1.50
DEAR LAURA *Jean Stubbs*	P2062	$1.25
THE IMPLOSION CONSPIRACY *Louis Nizer*	X2048	$1.75
NETHERGATE *Norah Lofts*	P2049	$1.25
THE SOVEREIGN STATE OF ITT		
Anthony Sampson	X2050	$1.75
A SURGEON'S WORLD *William A. Nolen, M.D.*	Q1996	$1.50
SNOWFIRE *Phyllis A. Whitney*	P2041	$1.25
GREEN DARKNESS *Anya Seton*	X2030	$1.75
THE SEARCH FOR A SOUL: THE PSYCHIC		
LIVES OF TAYLOR CALDWELL *Jess Stearn*	P2031	$1.75
STRANGERS IN COMPANY *Jane Aiken Hodge*	P2032	$1.25
SPEAK TO ME OF LOVE *Dorothy Eden*	P2014	$1.25
THE BEST AND THE BRIGHTEST		
David Halberstam	C2005	$1.95
THE ARM AND THE DARKNESS		
Taylor Caldwell	Q2006	$1.50
FREE AND FEMALE *Barbara Seaman*	Q1878	$1.50
THE OTHER *Thomas Tryon*	P1668	$1.25

Wherever Paperbacks Are Sold

If your bookdealer is sold out, send cover price plus 25¢ each for postage and handling to Mail Order Department, Fawcett Publications, Inc., P.O. Box 1014, Greenwich, Connecticut 06830. Please order by number and title. Catalog available on request.